Spinner

Spinner

Anthony Masters

BLACKIE CHILDREN'S BOOKS

To my friends Roger and Pat Dennien, whose work at Northease
Manor School near Lewes, East Sussex, has inspired me so much
and
to the Helen Allison School, Longfield Road, Meopham, Kent,
with many thanks for their assistance in writing this book.

BLACKIE CHILDREN'S BOOKS

Published by the Penguin Group
Penguin Books Ltd, 27 Wrights Lane, London W8 5TZ, England
Penguin Books USA Inc., 375 Hudson Street, New York, New York 10014, USA
Penguin Books Australia Ltd, Ringwood, Victoria, Australia
Penguin Books Canada Ltd, 10 Alcorn Avenue, Toronto, Ontario, Canada M4V 3B2
Penguin Books (NZ) Ltd, 182–190 Wairau Road, Auckland 10, New Zealand

Penguin Books Ltd, Registered Offices: Harmondsworth, Middlesex, England

First published 1993
1 3 5 7 9 10 8 6 4 2
First edition

Text copyright © Anthony Masters, 1993

Typeset by Datix International Limited, Bungay, Suffolk
Set in 13/15 pt Garamond
Printed in England by Clays Ltd, St Ives plc

A CIP catalogue record for this book is available from the British Library

ISBN 0–216–93270–X

Chapter One

The boy next door was spinning like a top and Jane watched him with a combination of fascinated interest and vague uneasiness. Was he crazy? And how was he able to keep it up for so long without getting dizzy or being sick? She went on staring at him from her kitchen door, while he spun round and round in the next-door back garden under the cloudless blue sky of a late June afternoon.

Then, quite suddenly, he stopped and fell down on the rather scrubby grass, his face turned up to the orange sun. He was about twelve, with short blond hair, a snub nose and a stocky body. Jane, who was about the same age, thought he was rather good-looking and wondered what his name was.

The family – or, at least, just the boy and his mother – had moved in a few days ago and hadn't introduced themselves. But why should they, Jane reasoned. No one would want to introduce themselves to Mum and Dad, who always looked so played out when they weren't drinking and who seemed so belligerent when they were. Anyway, no one introduced anyone to anyone on the Bell Farm Estate, because no one wanted to know anyone –

unless they might do them a bit of good, and that always led to trouble in the end.

Still, she would have liked to know this boy, spinning or not, and Jane wondered how she could. She wasn't very good at striking up conversations because she was shy, and she also knew that her parents wouldn't want anyone brought into the house. She wouldn't want to anyway; it was a tip.

Jane looked around her at the decaying gardens, the heaps of scrap and old prams at the bottom of most of them and the rusting cars at the kerbside. Some of them were burnt out; others were without wheels or windows – only a few actually seemed to go. There was more old junk on the pavements and graffiti everywhere. No one cared about Bell Farm – not the Council or the residents or the welfare or the social workers or anyone. The place was a dump, and that word exactly explained everything. All the problem families were dumped here by the Council – like Jane and her warring parents, who shouted and drank and fought and sulked around her twenty-four hours a day. They had moved dozens of times, always because they couldn't pay the rent, and now Dad was out of work again, Mum was an office cleaner and Jane bunked off school as much as she could because she hated it even more than home. Mostly she lay on her bed reading – she could escape into books – or watched endless daytime soap operas on TV. Her parents moaned at her for not going to school and a couple of times her dad had beaten her, so sometimes Jane pretended to go. Instead she got off the bus and mooched around Crawley, but as she had nothing to spend it was as boring as home or school. That was how she'd been nicked by the police, pinching food from the supermarket, and now the social workers were threatening to put her into care and for the first time she was really scared.

'Oi.'

Jane summoned up the courage to speak to the boy at last, but he didn't reply and simply lay staring up at the hard bright orb of the sun. There was no expression on his face at all.

'Oi,' she said again.

There was still no reply and he didn't move. Jane had the strange, fleeting idea that the boy's body was somehow parked, that it was only an outward shell and that he – the real person inside – had slipped away somehow. Maybe in the spinning. Then she shook herself. She must be potty, thinking weird thoughts like this.

'Oi,' she repeated impatiently for the third time. 'I'm talking to you.'

Jane's voice was threatening. She had inherited her dad's temper and thought nothing of getting into fights with other girls – or boys. In fact she quite enjoyed them, for she usually won and the violence was exciting, breaking the monotony of her life. Jane was tall for twelve, with a shock of dark brown hair in curly ringlets and a big, square, haunted face. She dressed like a boy as much as possible, usually in dirty T-shirts, tight jeans and trainers. She liked to think of herself as a rebel for, as with the fighting, the identity seemed to make her more of a personality.

'I said I'm talking to you.' She went to the fence and rapped on it angrily. At once the boy's eyes became startled and he rolled over and stood up.

7

'Only trying to be friendly,' Jane muttered.

For a moment he froze, and then with little scurrying jerky movements he ran for the cover of his house, banging the kitchen door behind him.

Chapter
Two

Later that evening, having grudgingly gone up to the paper shop for Dad, Jane thought she heard a funny kind of rattling in next door's garden and went over to see what it was. She was glad to be out, for her parents weren't speaking again. Dad had spent Mum's club money on a bottle of Scotch, and you could have cut the atmosphere in the house with a knife it was that thick.

Out here, under the stars, she felt refreshed – and curious about the weird noise. It was a warm night with a sickle moon and Jane could smell the nettles that grew around the broken tyres and old lavatory cistern that lay at the bottom of the jungle-like garden. Neither Dad nor Mum had the energy or the interest to tame the wilderness, and although Jane had sometimes been tempted to have a go, she had never actually got round to it. But she often came to stand here, because it was good to get out of the house and she loved the gleaming dark canopy of the night sky.

The rattling sound had a certain rhythm to it but at first she couldn't make out where it was coming from. Then, when she saw the strange shape in next door's garden, she knew what the sound was. In the shadowed half light a large barrel was rolling about on its side. Both ends were open and inside was an insubstantial form. Gradually she recognized it as the boy next door.

'What on earth do you think you're doing?' she whispered. As last time, there was no reply and Jane repeated her question fiercely. 'What on earth do you think you're doing?'

The barrel stopped rolling and the boy emerged. He looked tousled but there was still no expression on his face. Then he spoke. 'I was rolling.'

'Rolling? What for?'

'I like it. I like rolling.' His voice was curiously flat and, like his face, without expression. It also had a slightly mechanical quality to it and Jane felt both shocked and thrown.

'You were spinning earlier.'

'I like that spinning.'

He stared at her over the low fence as if he was looking through her rather than at her. It was curiously as if she didn't exist – as if she was a disembodied voice that he was only responding to because what she had said pleased him in some way.

Jane decided to change the subject, which clearly wasn't going anywhere.

'Where you from?'

'Kent.'

'Just you and your mum?' she asked probingly.

'We left my dad behind,' he said monotonously. 'He's a cowboy.'

'What?'

'He's a cowboy.'

'In Kent?'

He stared straight ahead without speaking. It was as if he had completely lost interest.

'What's your name? Mine's Jane, Jane Lomax.'

'Gary Bird,' he intoned. 'I'm twelve and I live at – I live at 14 Birch Drive.'

'I know that, you prat,' snapped Jane. 'I'm your next-door neighbour, remember.'

Gary didn't reply. She could sense that he was going to turn on his heel at any moment and march indoors, so she quickly asked him another question.

'Is that your dad's job – being a cowboy?'

'Yes.'

'How can he – oh, never mind.'

Then Gary actually volunteered a statement. 'I'm going home.'

'You *are* at home.'

'I'm going to my dad.'

'Where is he?'

'Kent.'

'Oh yeah? What, for a holiday or something?' Obviously Gary's parents had split up, thought Jane.

'No.'

'Then –'

'I'm going for ever.' Gary smiled for an instant, but the smile had vanished so quickly that Jane wasn't sure if it had been there in the first place. Maybe it hadn't. 'I don't like it here.'

'Why?'

'The school. I don't like the school.'

'Which school?'

'St Bede's.'

'That's the special school,' Jane blurted out, 'for mentally –' Just in time she stopped herself, although there wasn't the slightest sign that Gary understood what she had been going to say. So that was it, she thought. That explained the spinning and the rolling. Gary was mental.

'So you're going to run away then?'

Gary stared at her, looking uneasy and puzzled. 'I'm going to my dad's,' he repeated doggedly.

'With your mum?'

'No.'

'Then you're going to run away, aren't you?' snapped Jane. 'Stands to reason.' But she soon realized that reason didn't come into it – not with Gary. She was sure of that.

Chapter
Three

Gary stared at her and then ran in without saying goodbye, leaving Jane gazing at the barrel. What a nutter, she said to herself, glancing across at the silent house next door. Then she, too, went inside, to find her mother sitting in the kitchen with her head in her hands and Dad in the sitting-room, flat out and snoring in front of the telly. What a mess, she thought, glancing round the untidy rooms with their litter of dirty plates and cups and crumpled weeks-old newspapers. What a life. But it was better being here in the pigsty than being in care. The two words struck an awful all-pervading chill in her heart. In care – it sounded like a life sentence. Mum and Dad might not make much of a home for her but at least she had her room and her privacy. The sudden image of a long, long dormitory with rows of iron bedsteads and a hatchet-faced matron flashed into her mind. The scene was probably culled from something she'd seen on telly, but as Jane didn't really understand what being in care was it was an image that seemed to mean something – and mean something very unpleasant indeed.

She went up and lay on her bed. The social worker was going to see her parents some time next week and

Jane knew how worried her mother was. She had tried hard to control her drinking recently, but it had been difficult with Dad out of work and so bitter that he drank much more heavily than she in a desperate attempt to blot out his worries. But he always woke up with a hangover next morning and his problems just as bad, if not worse, than the night before.

Tomorrow was Saturday and Jane tried to dismiss the future from her mind. She had planned to go into Crawley with her friend Sue and walk round the shops. It wouldn't be much of an outing as she had done it so many times on her own when she was bunking off school, but at least she'd be with someone and be able to talk.

Jane undressed and got into bed, willing sleep to come – as quite often it didn't. But tonight she felt quite drowsy, and as she slipped into a deeper sleep Jane saw Gary spinning again and later she dreamt that she was in his garden, spinning with him.

The next morning was even hotter, and as Jane went downstairs to make herself some breakfast the day yawned before her, long and boring and, even with Sue's company, absolutely empty. Then she saw that even the larder was bare – no cereal, no bread, no milk, no anything. Jane groaned; she would have to go down to the little Spar supermarket on the edge of the estate and put it on the bill that she suspected was already vastly overdue. Oh well – She opened the front door and looked out at the sunny, crummy street. Somehow Bell Farm looked even more tatty than usual in the sharp sunlight, and there was a left-over staleness to the road and the houses outside that really depressed her. She set out, ignoring the wolf-whistling of the paper-boy, conscious for once that she looked a right mess in her dirty old T-shirt and jeans.

Something was going on when she arrived at the battered little supermarket. There was a crowd of people wedged in the front, blocking the check-out, and rearing up above all of them was Mrs Mountford, the huge and roughly spoken local teacher who was Jane's form tutor and who was always going on about her – inevitably to her detriment.

'Well,' she said as Jane pushed her way curiously through the crowd, 'here's a child who causes as much disruption as you do.'

'Oh yeah?'

'It's outrageous. Where's his mother? And what on earth's the matter with the lad?'

'Blimey.' Now that Jane could see what was going on, she didn't know whether to laugh, or try to stop him. Gary was standing on a large crate in one of the aisles of the supermarket, piling egg-boxes one on top of the other until he had achieved a shaky-looking skyscraper. Judging by everyone's expression, thought Jane, they must be full of eggs.

Chapter
Four

'Look, my lad,' said the manager, trying to speak calmly, 'just stop that, do you hear?'

But Gary didn't; he carried on, carefully piling laden box on laden box until the tower soared to the ceiling, miraculously intact. But for how long? wondered Jane. How long? Meanwhile the manager stood stock still, watching him guardedly as if he was dangerous, and when Jane looked round at the other shoppers she detected the same fear in them. Gary was purposeful, expressionless, odd-looking – and his body language certainly had its effect in keeping everyone at bay.

'He's on drugs,' muttered someone.

'Them speed-ups,' said someone else. 'That's what it is – he's hooked.'

'More like a nutter.'

'Someone get the police.'

'Did you hear me?' quavered the manager. 'You're not to do that.'

But still he remained where he was, not moving a step forward, as if he was frozen in time and space. Jane wondered if *she* ought to do something. But what? What was there to do? Gary seemed so grimly intent on his task that she was sure he would be very upset if he was interrupted. There was a great intensity in his stare and a total absorption in what he was doing – as if Gary was living in one world with his egg-boxes and Jane and the spectators were living in another.

'They're going to fall,' hissed Mrs Mountford. But they didn't and Gary went on building higher and higher. Then Jane saw someone pushing through the crowd – someone who looked purposeful and calm. She was a tall, thin woman in her thirties with a tired, pale face and strands of fair hair that she kept pushing back out of her eyes. At once Jane could see the likeness and was sure that this must be Gary's mother.

The woman paused and then moved quietly forward. 'Gary,' she said softly.

He went on building.

'Gary.'

Still he went on building and she advanced a little further.

'Gary.'

He looked up balefully. 'Busy,' he said in an abstracted voice.

'Time to go home,' she pronounced gently.

'Busy,' Gary repeated firmly.

'We've got to get home.'

Then the manager, more confident now he had seen them talking, pushed past her. 'You stop that, lad, and now.'

'No,' she whispered. 'Don't talk to him like that.'

'No?' he repeated very indignantly. 'What do you mean *no*? Who are you?' He turned on the woman aggressively.

'I'm his mother.'

'What are you doing, allowing him to behave like this?'

'I left my purse at home,' she explained to the manager with a slow dignity. 'I asked him to wait by the entrance. He doesn't usually go into shops on his own. Maybe he was hot.'

As they talked, Jane's nerves screamed as she watched Gary build his pile of egg-boxes higher and miraculously higher. Would they never fall? she wondered. Was Gary practising some kind of magic?

'And he usually behaves like this?' asked the manager threateningly.

'He's handicapped,' the woman said quietly.

'In what way?' boomed Mrs Mountford officiously from behind, and Jane hated her for her interference.

'He's autistic.'

'Does that mean he's dangerous?' asked someone.

'No.' The woman flushed. 'Of course it doesn't mean that. He's – he's mentally handicapped.'

'Ah.' The manager's voice took on a sepulchral tone. 'I see.'

There was a long silence during which Gary added one more egg-box. Sadly it was one too many and the pile – the whole edifice – began to sway and totter.

'Stop him,' howled the manager, about to lose all control. 'Just *stop* him.'

'It's too late,' whispered Jane, speaking for the first time.

In slow motion, the boxes fell in a series of miniature explosions. Shells cracked, eggs tumbled and egg-yolk spread everywhere in a rain of vivid yellow. As the devastation occurred, Gary gave a howl of primeval rage and jumped off his crate. Then he began to stamp

18

up and down in the mess, shouting and crying and sobbing.

'This is outrageous,' said the manager. 'You know you'll have to pay for all this.' He turned in a rage on Gary's mother but she ignored him, slowly and quietly walking over the liquid floor to the screaming and egg-stained Gary.

'Come on, love,' she said. 'It's all OK.'

'I beg your pardon, madam?' spluttered the manager.

'Well, really,' commented Mrs Mountford. 'There's just no home discipline these days. How can parents expect –'

'I'll settle up later,' said Gary's mother. 'Now I'm taking him home.' Although he was still yelling, she took her son's hand and led him out of the super-market. Jane didn't think she had seen anyone quite so dignified in her life.

Chapter
Five

Jane couldn't keep Gary out of her mind all the time she was window-shopping with Sue, and it was with some relief that she finally parted with her. On the way home she suddenly realized to her surprise that she actually wanted to see Gary. The eggs episode in the supermarket had moved her very deeply, and she was curious about him. What kind of mental handicap made this boy spin like a top, roll around in barrels, build skyscrapers with egg-boxes? It was weird; in fact it was more than weird – it was extraordinary.

Both her parents were out when she got in and the house was in its usual disgusting mess. Still thinking about Gary, she made a half-hearted attempt to clean up the living-room. Later she made herself a cup of tea, only to find that once again there was no milk. So – here was a heaven-sent opportunity for nipping round next door. She longed to know what Gary was doing – what he would get up to next. In Jane's predictable and boring life Gary had become a star. Also, there was something in the back of her mind that she wouldn't admit to herself properly, at least not yet. In fact Jane was wondering if there was any way she could help him; the thought hovered in her subconscious, making her feel warm and hopeful.

Slowly she walked round to the front of the Birds' house and rather hesitantly knocked on the door. There was a long delay before the door opened and, feeling unusually nervous, Jane was just about to knock again when Mrs Bird suddenly stood on the threshold. She looked thin and drained.

'Yes?'

'I'm your next-door neighbour – Jane Lomax.' She knew she sounded horribly bright and tried unsuccessfully to be more casual. 'Er – I wonder if I could borrow some milk.'

'Hang on.' To Jane's disappointment she didn't invite her in but plunged back into the depths of the house. She could smell frying and hear the murmur of a television set. Then Mrs Bird returned with a bottle of milk and a blank expression on her face. Her body gave off vibrations of minor impatience. 'I can spare a pint.'

'Thanks.'

Mrs Bird was about to shut the door firmly when Jane said, 'Er – '

'Yes?'

'How's Gary?'

'Very well, thank you.' Her voice was clipped and bland.

'I saw him in the supermarket.'

'Oh yes?'

'When he was piling the eggs up.'

'Ah.'

'I want to help pay for them.'

'What?' Mrs Bird stared at her as if she must be mad and Jane herself was very surprised. Now what on earth had made her say that? She had no money anyway.

'I'd like to help pay.'

'There's no need.' Her voice was even more expressionless than before.

'I'm not trying to be patronizing.'

'No?'

They both paused, having reached total impasse.

'Can I see Gary?' asked Jane desperately.

'Why?'

'I'd – I'd like to get to know him.'

'No one can do that.' She sounded matter of fact, impossibly smug.

'Why not?'

'He's handicapped.'

'I know,' said Jane. 'I mean – I know that.'

'Oh yes?'

'What kind of – what sort of –' She didn't know how to say it or how to end it, suddenly feeling absurd, standing on this woman's doorstep, clutching a pint of borrowed milk.

'He's autistic.'

'What does that mean?'

'It means Gary is very self-absorbed – very interested in himself. He doesn't communicate and he doesn't respond to people, so I don't see any point in you –'

'We've already met,' said Jane quietly.

'Oh yes?' It was clearly her favourite expression.

'He was playing in the garden.'

'Oh yes.'

If anyone doesn't communicate, thought Jane with a feeling of intense irritation, it's his mother. 'So I can't see him?'

'I didn't say can't. Look, here he is.'

Gary was standing behind her, in the back of the hallway. Jane hadn't heard him arrive, and the shadows were so deep that she hadn't seen him. It was rather eerie, as if he had suddenly materialized.

'Hi, Gary.'

There was no reply.

'Hallo.'

Still no response.

'See what I mean?' said his mother.

'Is he always like that?' whispered Jane.

'Don't worry – you can talk in front of him.' She seemed marginally more friendly, as if Gary's appearance had somehow proved his handicap by so effectively putting it on show. For some reason that seemed to please Mrs Bird. 'Yes, he's always like that, but he's depressed too now,' her voice droned.

'Depressed?'

'Missing his dad.'

'He told me – or at least he said he was going to see him – that his dad was –'

'Told you quite a bit, hasn't he?'

'Well –' I thought you said he didn't communicate, thought Jane slowly.

'Anyway, it's all a load of rubbish.'

Gary was still standing there, staring past them.

'He can't go anywhere.'

There was another silence but Mrs Bird showed no sign of leaving the doorstep. Maybe she doesn't usually speak to anyone, thought Jane. Maybe this conversation, however weird and stumbling, is doing her good.

'His dad and I have split up; we came here from Kent.'

'He told me that too – and that he's going to a special school he doesn't like.'

'He'll tell you some things,' she admitted, 'but he may never do it again.'

'I'd still like to see him,' said Jane.

'Why?'

'I like him.'

There was another long pause. 'He misses his dad, but I had to come away. It was no good between us.' She looked behind her. 'So they put us here – while we sort ourselves out.'

'Won't he see his dad?'

'Bad blood between me and him. His dad's violent – used to knock me around. He doesn't even know we're here.'

'Please let me see him.' Jane now had a very sure instinct that she should go in and make more contact, but she didn't really know why.

Grudgingly Mrs Bird stood aside. 'Come in and make what you can of him then. Besides, it'll be nice to have a bit of company.' Suddenly she seemed to unbend a little. 'That supermarket business fair shook me up. That's just the sort of thing he would go and do.'

As Jane entered the house, Mrs Bird half smiled at her, as if she was suddenly pleased that Jane had practically forced her way in. She must be terribly lonely, thought Jane. Just stuck with Gary.

'I'd like to help pay,' she repeated. 'I hope I haven't upset you.'

'No, it's a nice thought.'
And that's all it is, thought Jane ruefully.

Chapter
Six

She walked into an untidy sitting-room which had a pile of toy building bricks in the centre. They were built up to a considerable height.

'Egg-boxes again,' muttered Jane.

Mrs Bird nodded. 'It's one of his obsessions; something he has to do all day. Build up those bricks. He's been like it since he was a baby.'

'That and the spinning and the barrel-rolling,' observed Jane.

'Yes, but it's all got worse since we left Kent, and he doesn't half get into tantrums.' She looked at Gary as if he was an object she didn't want to touch. Then Jane saw the love come back into Mrs Bird's eyes. 'Oh well,' she said, 'he's a cross I have to bear and he'll get used to the new school. It was a wrench for him leaving his home and his dad and his old school, I'll grant you that. But I couldn't stay. No, not with him.' She lowered her voice. 'Dave was a brute, a real brute to me.'

'Did he hurt Gary?' asked Jane hesitantly.

'No – not him. He was the apple of Dave's eye – couldn't do no wrong. They say autistic kids can't relate to anyone – don't miss anyone – but he's missing

Dave all right.' Mrs Bird paused. 'Course it may not *just* be Dave.'

'What do you mean?'

'Gary likes to control everything he does – or try to. His dad built him a house.'

'A what?'

'Only a tiny one. More like a Wendy house – you know what I mean. But it fits him like a glove.'

Jane couldn't believe what Mrs Bird was saying. 'You mean – Gary wears a house?'

'Almost.' She smiled. 'The school – the old school – said it wasn't any good for him – perpetuating obsessional behaviour or something – but Dave would insist. Gary calls the little house "Dunroamin".'

As she spoke Gary looked up from his bricks and repeated the word in his monotonous voice. 'Dunroamin – I want Dunroamin.' He broke off and returned to his bricks, piling up his skyscraper as carefully as he had done with the egg-boxes.

'S'pose he grows out of the house?' asked Jane reasonably.

'Oh, Dave can adjust that. He's good with his hands.'

'But what would happen when Gary grew up?'

'God knows. But he's here with me now. Dunroamin indeed – I ask you.'

'Gary said – said he was going to run away.'

Mrs Bird paused. 'I know,' she said unexpectedly.

'Could he?'

'I don't think so, but I know another autistic kid who ran home. Got there somehow; kind of homing instinct, like a pigeon. Kept asking till he got there I s'pose.' She looked worried as she stared down at him.

27

'He said his dad was a cowboy.'

Mrs Bird smiled. 'Dave was a waiter in the Texas Steak House in Margate. They have to dress up like that.' She paused again and muttered, as if to herself, 'Worships his dad, Gary does. Made me feel so cruel to go.' Then she looked Jane directly in the eye. 'But he was a brute. I was in a refuge with Gary, would you credit that?'

'What's a refuge?'

'Place for battered wives. Anyway, I'll leave you with him. Can't be gossiping all day – I've got a home to run.'

She went into the kitchen and began to rattle about, leaving Jane not knowing what to do or say to Gary.

She knelt down and looked at the bricks as Gary's deft hands picked them up and added them to the pile. She felt that if she breathed the column would tumble and Jane was sure that Gary would be furious. There was a look of deep concentration in his eyes as he went on adding brick after brick.

'It's stretching right up,' he said.

'Yes,' replied Jane dutifully.

'Stretching right up to heaven.'

'Yes.'

'I'll be able to get to Dad.'

Jane felt a thrill of shock seize her. 'Your dad's not in heaven.'

'Where is he then?'

'He's at home.'

'I want to go home,' said Gary. 'I want Dun-roamin.'

Jane picked up a brick involuntarily as she saw the tears in his eyes.

28

'I want Dunroamin,' he whispered. 'I'm going home.'

Then Gary saw that Jane was still offering him the brick and glared at her angrily. 'What's that for?'

'For your skyscraper,' she said gently.

'What?' There was a distinct edge to his voice.

'For your – your building. Your pile of –'

'Don't want it.' Gary was very fierce now.

Jane's uplifted hand froze and then she withdrew it with such a sudden rush of air that it was all too much for Gary's triumphant construction – and the bricks collapsed around them in a series of dull thuds. Momentarily, Jane felt the loss as keenly as Gary, as his castle or stairway to heaven or home or whatever he thought it was continued to rain down around them.

With a snarl, Gary turned on Jane and slapped her round the face – and then he did it again. 'See what you've done,' he bellowed in rage. 'See what you've gone and done.'

She cringed back from him as Mrs Bird ran into the room to see Gary's hand raised again and his face working frenziedly.

'Gary!'

He picked up a brick and then another and another and another. But instead of throwing them at Jane he threw them against the wall.

'Gary!' yelled Mrs Bird. 'Put those down.'

But he went on throwing the bricks.

Chapter
Seven

Jane did not see Gary for several days after the disaster of the building bricks. Mrs Bird had hurriedly shown her out of the house and she had felt completely bewildered as she left to the sound of more bricks thudding against the wall.

'That's why people don't get to know Gary,' Mrs Bird had told her almost triumphantly, as if she had wanted to prove her point. But there had been a sadness too, a weariness that had no doubt been born of years of Gary's tantrums, and now she had no one to share them with. It must be awful, thought Jane as she went through her dreary round of school and home, awful to be alone with him like that, not to be able to share him and his problem with anyone. Surely even the violent Dave might have been better than no one.

By the third day, Jane was so much on the lookout for Gary that she couldn't get him out of her mind, and she kept wandering out into the garden in the hope of seeing him spinning or rolling about in his barrel. But he didn't put in any appearance at all and, of course, it wasn't long before her parents started to comment.

'Mooning around, dreaming about,' was all her

father would really commit himself to, but her mother was more vocal and more mockingly probing.

Half drunk, half desperate for new experience or scandal, she said, 'It's that kid next door – the nutty one. I think she fancies him or something. I mean, he's not bad-looking, is he? Just loopy in the head.'

'Shut up, Mum.'

'Anyway,' continued her mother self-pityingly, 'she shows more interest in that dumbo than she does in me. Never helps – never cleans up after her. Look at the state of the place.'

Her mother rummaged in a drawer to find a hidden bottle and then discovered she had drunk it already. Cursing, she straightened up to moan even harder, but this time Dad joined in with Jane to yell, 'Oh, shut up.'

On the third evening, Jane disconsolately wandered out yet again into the garden and saw Gary spinning on the central patch of grass near his other next-door neighbour's clothes-line. He was a weird sight, like an alien who had just landed from outer space and wasn't yet quite out of orbit.

Then Gary stopped and came down to earth.

'Hi,' said Jane softly.

'Hallo. I'm Gary Bird. I live at –'

'Yes,' she replied. 'I know.'

But he frowned and continued, 'I live at 14 Birch Drive and I'm twelve years old.' His voice sounded even more like a computer but Jane thought she detected the warmth of recognition in his eyes. Or was it just her imagination? Probably it was, she thought grimly, for when she looked into his eyes again, Jane was sure she could only see blankness there.

Then he said something amazing. 'I'm going home.'

'You are home,' Jane replied woodenly, wondering if they were about to have a repeat performance of their earlier conversation.

'Real home.' He looked at her. 'Dunroamin.'

She didn't know what to say. Then she blurted out, 'Your mum – she won't want you to go.'

Gary stared through her. 'Dunroamin,' he said again.

'How will you get there?'

'Walk.'

'To Margate?'

Again he stared at her blankly. Clearly her questions made no impact on him at all.

'How will you know the way?' Jane persisted.

'I can ask my way,' said Gary in his articulate monotone. 'I can ask directions, can't I?'

'Er – yes. It's a long walk.'

'I can walk.'

'Yes.'

'I shall see my dad. At the end of the walk. My dad's a cowboy.'

'Is he?' She just didn't know what to say.

'He's a cowboy,' Gary repeated.

'Yes.'

'He has a gun. A gun in his holster. He made my Dunroamin.' Gary yawned. 'I'm going to my Dunroamin now.'

'Now?'

'Yes.'

'But you can't –' began Jane.

'Goodbye.'

Gary turned and walked down the narrow passageway that led between the back and front gardens of the houses. Jane followed him on her side of fence and they both met on the outside road at the same time.

'Gary!' She stood in front of him, barring his way, and he frowned. 'You can't just go off like this.'

'You're in the way.'

'You'll only get lost.'

'Go away.'

'I'll call your mother.'

'She's sleeping.'

Jane couldn't think what to do next; they were at a total impasse, but she knew that somehow she had to stop Gary embarking on his crazy journey.

'You can't go,' she repeated rather numbly. 'You'll get lost.'

'Go away.'

'Gary –'

'Go away.' His monotone was louder and his fists clenched. Jane looked desperately around her but the street was empty.

'I'm not letting you go anywhere. You'll only get lost or hurt or –'

There was a dead look of rage in Gary's eyes as he sprang at her, and the force of his sudden attack was so great that she fell over with him on top of her. Immediately she found that he was much stronger than she – much stronger than anyone she had ever fought with – and as Gary rained frantic blows on her face she tried to shield herself with her arms, kicking out ineffectively with her legs. He grabbed her head and banged it hard on the concrete path. Then he did it again.

*

Jane lay on the ground, dazed, her head hurting and tears of pain starting out of her eyes. She had not expected Gary to be so vicious and had been completely taken by surprise at his attack. She lay there for a few more seconds and then struggled unsteadily to her feet. There were a few passers-by now but no one offered to help her, and one or two people deliberately walked by on the other side. There was something in the Bible about this, she thought darkly, as she limped back towards Gary's house, her head splitting and her anger increasing. That little beast; she'd get him, however handicapped he was.

Chapter
Eight

Jane knocked at Mrs Bird's front door time and time again but there was no reply. Gary had said she was asleep but this was the sleep of the dead. Eventually she heard the sound of dragging feet, and the door opened reluctantly.

'Mrs Bird.'

'Mm?' She looked awful, her face pale and her hair unkempt.

'It's me.'

'Me?'

'Jane.'

'Who?'

'Jane, next door.'

'What do you want? I was asleep.'

Her head was still ringing with pain but Jane yelled, 'Gary.'

'What about him? He's indoors somewhere.'

'He's not. He's gone.'

'Gone?' She looked at her, utterly bewildered. 'I was asleep. Took a pill because I haven't been sleeping nights. And then you came knocking and –'

'Mrs Bird, Gary's gone. He's run away.'

'He's in his room. I know he is.' Her voice was

defensive.

'He's not now. He's run away. Mrs Bird – we've *got* to stop him.'

Mrs Bird looked wildly around her and abruptly took action at last, darting round the house and then hurrying back, her eyes wide with alarm. 'He's gone and done it – the little – he's upped and gone.'

'Hadn't you better call the police?'

'Yes. I expect he's only a few streets away, but –'

'But what?'

'It's happened before,' she wailed.

'What?'

'I left Dave a couple of years ago – only moved two or three miles away –'

'And Gary walked home?' Jane finished for her impatiently.

Mrs Bird nodded miserably. 'God knows how, but he did.'

'Will he speak to strangers?'

'Only if he has to.'

'Will they think him odd?' asked Jane hesitantly.

'You bet your sweet life they will,' she replied fervently. 'How would you react if you were approached by a boy with a monotone voice who wanted to know the way to Margate – from Crawley?' She gave a slightly hysterical laugh and then edged away inside. 'I'm going to ring the police,' she said. 'I'm sure they'll soon head him off.'

Jane nodded. 'I'll take a look round – see if I can find him.'

'Be careful,' said Mrs Bird quickly. 'Gary can be very violent when he's thwarted.'

'I know that already,' replied Jane with feeling.

*

36

Jane searched the darkening summer streets with no success. There was absolutely no sign of Gary anywhere as she roved through road after road of little brick houses, some with Tudor gables and others square-fronted, their windows staring out at her like sightless eyes. The air smelt of petrol fumes and hot tar, with a whiff of hot dog and onions as she neared the town centre. Which way would Gary go for Margate on foot? Which way would *anyone* go for Margate on foot?

Her head was still sore and ached a lot, but rather than hating him for what he had done to her, Jane merely felt a desperate longing to see him. She had a fixed mental image of Gary, walking confidently towards Dunroamin, asking toneless questions, a total innocent at the mercy of anyone and everyone.

Eventually Jane returned home and knocked at Mrs Bird's front door. This time it was opened immediately and Jane could hardly bear the frantic look of hope in Mrs Bird's eyes.

'I haven't seen him,' Jane said bluntly.

'The police are looking.' She gave a hopeless little sigh. 'There's nothing else we can do.'

'No.'

'You'd better go back.'

Jane felt hurt at being dismissed. Somehow she had felt part of Gary's life when she was looking for him. Now she was nothing.

'I'll let you know what happens,' Mrs Bird called after her, but Jane still felt excluded. It would have been so much nicer if she had asked her into the house to wait with her, to be part of the drama. To return to

Mum and Dad was too dreary and hopeless to be contemplated. She would set out again and continue to search for Gary – and she wouldn't come back until she had found him. With this forlorn hope in mind, Jane set out for the second time, her feet now aching as much as her head.

Jane wandered the darkening streets for the next hour, sure that Gary was widening the distance between them each minute. She still tried to think of the direction he might take, but inwardly she knew that it was all hopeless and that very soon it would be too dark to search and she would have to go back to the bleak living-room of her house and wait.

Suddenly she saw the gates to the park and paused. This wasn't the kind of place she would ever have wanted to approach at twilight, let alone after dark, but still she waited, trying to see beyond the gates. It wasn't very big, just a square of grass, maybe a quarter of an acre, with a fence around it. There was a dried-out ornamental pond, a little café with a few battered chairs and tables outside, and a children's sandpit that she knew lay somewhere behind it. The park was the haunt of down-and-outs and young boys and girls who were unemployed and had nowhere to go. It was a sad, desolate little place – just as bad as the estate that she lived on.

The café was hung with rusty Coca-Cola signs and had an even more desolate air to it than the park, but there were signs of life – an old man was folding up the flimsy-looking tables, whistling to himself, a re-assuring presence in the shadowy darkness. Jane wandered in and walked up to him.

38

'We're closing,' he said, shifting the cigarette between his lips a little to allow speech. 'You can't come in now.'

'I want to ask you a question.'

'A question?' Immediately he looked suspicious. 'I don't want no questions. You clear off – we're closing. And I'm going to shift that other little pest if it's the last thing I do.'

'*Other* little pest?'

'Perishing mental kid in the sandpit. Won't listen, won't speak. Making a tower or something, isn't he? I'll ask him one more time and then I'll sling him out on his ear. Sauce.'

'Wait – wait a minute,' Jane gasped, her pulse racing.

'Well?'

'I know him.'

'*Know* him?' The man put down the table and stared at her angrily. 'If you know him – shift him.'

'That might not be so easy.' But she was tremendously elated all the same. The boy in the sandpit must be Gary. He *must* be. 'Can I see him?' she said eagerly.

'It's public property – he's round the back.'

Jane hurried round to the rear of the shabby little café and stood stock still in wonderment. Gary was crouched down in the sandpit. He had a fire bucket of water which was marked WEST SUSSEX COUNTY COUNCIL, and he was using it to dampen the sand – with which he was making the thinnest and tallest tower she had ever seen. It soared up into the night sky like a needle pointing – pointing to Margate. Gary was concentrating hard, building it higher and higher with his painstakingly wetted sand.

39

'Gary.'

He ignored her, she didn't even know whether he had heard her.

'Gary. It's me, Jane.'

Still he ignored her.

'When you've finished I've come to take you home.'

Gary hummed a monotonous, unmelodious little tune. 'I'm going to Dunroamin – to Margate. I'm going to see my dad.'

'Come home – we can go tomorrow.'

'I'm going now.'

'Tomorrow?' she repeated hopelessly, knowing she would have to go to a call-box and telephone the police. They would be able to deal with him. She couldn't; he was far too strong for her and she didn't want a repetition of the last bout of violence. But would he stay? Would the little man with the cigarette *allow* him to stay? She would have to go and convince him. Maybe there was a phone in the café.

'Will you be staying here long?' she asked as calmly as she could, but Gary didn't reply and simply went on wetting and shaping the sand and adding to his tower until it was as precariously high as the egg-boxes in the supermarket or the bricks in his front room. She was sure that quite soon there would be a calamity and then it would be time for an angry Gary to move on.

Without saying anything, Jane edged away. She was just about to return to the front of the café when she heard a very curious grunting and spluttering that instinctively made her stop where she was.

Then she heard a voice, low and agitated: 'Hit him again.'

Chapter
Nine

When she peered round the front of the café the old man was lying on the grass and she could see that a stream of blood was pouring down his forehead and towards his mouth. Two boys were standing over him. They were dressed in tight oily jeans and motorcycle gear.

'You should never have hit him with your helmet, Angel,' said the podgier, squatter of the two. The other boy was tall and slight, but there was something about him that really terrified Jane. The light of the wan café neon illuminated a livid scar that ran down one side of his face, but it wasn't the scar that terrified her; it was his smile. The boy looked as if he didn't have a care in the world, and as if he wouldn't care for anybody in it.

Angel had a tin box in his hand and out of it he pulled a wad of notes. He gave a low whistle. 'Nice one.'

'How much?'

'All right – I can't count at the speed of light, can I? Just be patient, Ed.' Jane thought his voice sounded odd; it was much more educated than she would have expected, but it was almost as if he was trying to roughen it out. 'Best part of two grand,' he added.

Ed grunted, part thrilled, part horrified by what they had done. He bent down and put his ear to the old man's chest. 'He's breathing bad.'

'Ring an ambulance. There's a box on the corner.'

'You ought never to have hit him like that.'

'Shut up and go and phone.'

'I can't –'

'Go and phone, Ed. Now.'

'S'pose someone comes?'

'I'll be all right,' replied Angel quietly.

'Yeah – you'll do a runner, won't you? With the money like.'

'Go and phone. I'll be here.' Angel's voice was authoritative.

'How do I know?'

'How long we been together, Ed? I'm not doing any runners on you. Now get to that call-box. Fast.'

Despite her fear Jane was curious; once again she had the distinct impression that Angel was posh playing down, but her main thought was concentrated on how she and Gary could remain hidden and not receive the attentions of the boy.

She glanced back but there was no sign of Gary yet. Please God let him go on building his tower. Please God don't let it fall down. And please God, Ed, get on with it and hurry back soon. She did spare a thought for the old man and wondered bleakly if he would die.

Ed lumbered off while Angel started to count the money. Occasionally he glanced down at the old man, who was now breathing in a very ragged way, but there was something in his gaze that really chilled Jane

– for Angel looked as if he was staring at something on the supermarket shelf.

Eventually, after what seemed like hours, Ed came back.

'We gotta go. They're on their way.' He looked down at the old man. 'He's bad.' Ed was both terrified and confused. 'You still counting that money?'

'Fancy him keeping all this in there,' said Angel calmly, still counting each note carefully. 'These old fools – don't trust the banks, do they?'

'Come *on*!' Ed was beside himself with frustration.

'Yeah, yeah.'

'They'll be here!'

'OK.' He shoved the notes into the pocket of his jerkin. 'Let's go.'

Gary pushed past Jane as Ed and Angel were walking through the gates of the park to a couple of motor-bikes. She had been so intent on what was happening in front of the café that she hadn't heard his purposeful tread.

'Stop,' she whispered, trying to push him back, but as usual he was too strong for her.

'Go away,' Gary said loudly. 'I'm going to Margate.'

'Your tower – the sandpit –'

'It's finished now.' He hurried briskly out to the front of the café, literally stepped over the old man and, spotting the retreating backs of Angel and Ed, called out robotically, 'Excuse me.'

'What the hell?' Ed turned back at once and Angel also whipped round with that lethal smile of his. The smile widened as he saw Gary.

'What do you want?'

'I want to know the way to Margate please,' said Gary politely. 'Can you tell me which way I go?'

'Blimey,' said Ed. 'He's seen us. He's a witness. Come on, let's . . .'

The sound of an ambulance siren cleaved the night air as Gary repeated, 'Excuse me, do you know the way to Margate?'

Jane then made the fatal mistake of coming out of the shadows. She knew she had to protect Gary and acted entirely by instinct, but it was a move she was to regret for the rest of her life.

'Who the hell are you?' asked Angel, the smile rigid on his thin face.

'You leave him alone,' blurted out Jane. 'Just leave him.' She glanced down at the body of the old man and then met Angel's eyes again. They were cold, mocking steel but there was something else in them that made her start to shiver.

The ambulance siren increased in volume and Ed yelled, 'For heaven's sake, Angel –'

Angel stared deep into Jane's eyes. 'You describe me – and I'll kill you. Do you understand?'

'I'll describe you all right,' she said, a blind bravery suddenly coming over her. 'You brute, look what you've done to that old man – just for a little bit of money.'

Angel's eyes were hard. 'I'll find you,' he said in his silky posh voice. 'I'll find you wherever you are. And I'll kill you.'

'Excuse me,' said Gary for the third time. He spoke with gathering impatience. 'Excuse me, but can you tell me the way to Margate?'

*

Angel and Ed ran to their motor-bikes, leapt on to them and roared off into the night, leaving Jane and Gary standing in front of the café. She thought fast and grabbed Gary's arm, which was rock hard with indignation.

'He didn't tell me —'

'Listen, we can't stay here. We've got to run.'

'But he didn't tell me the way to Margate.'

'Shut up!'

'Don't be rude,' Gary told her sanctimoniously. 'Don't be so rude.'

Jane controlled herself with an effort. 'We've got to run away.'

'Why?'

'Those boys killed an old man and the ambulance is coming. They'll think *we* did it.'

'Who will?' he asked without curiosity.

'The police, the ambulance men — I don't know. But — but —' Then she had an inspiration. 'But if we don't run, you'll never get to Margate.'

'I don't want to go with you,' he said, standing rooted to the spot, and Jane nearly screamed in frustration.

'You've *got* to,' she snapped.

'No.'

Then she had another brilliant idea. 'I *know* the way to Margate.'

'You do?'

'Yes.'

'You know the way to Margate?'

'Of course I do.' Jane thought desperately. 'It's easy — the way to Margate's easy.'

'Dunroamin,' said Gary excitedly and she noticed a

note of warmth in his voice for the first time. 'I want to be in Dunroamin.'

'You will be,' said Jane with a confidence that she didn't feel. 'But it's going to be a long walk.' Now she knew that she had to go with him, had to find the way herself, for if she did she would at least be able to keep him in sight. Of course she could telephone and alert the police so they could pick him up, but suddenly she didn't want to; she wanted to be with Gary on his journey and to find his Dunroamin. Why, she hadn't the faintest idea; all she knew was that for the first time in years she had a goal that filled her with immense pleasure.

Then the feeling of heady idealistic happiness came down to earth with a bump as she remembered Angel's words: 'I'll find you. I'll find you wherever you are. And I'll kill you.' The silky posh voice ran on in her head.

Chapter
Ten

'All right then,' said Gary.

'You agree?'

'You know the way. I'll come with *you*.' He sounded commanding. 'I could get on with my tower for a bit if you want to think.'

'I *don't* want to think.' The howl of the ambulance was coming up the street. 'Let's run round the back – there's a hole in the fence.'

'I don't go through holes,' said Gary brightly and firmly. 'They spoil my clothes.'

'You will if you want to get to Margate,' replied Jane, improvising swiftly. 'Now hold my hand and run.'

Obediently, Gary thrust a rigid hand in hers and they ran.

Hand in hand they ran through the back streets for about ten minutes. Gary was stiff and awkward as they pounded the pavements, but once she got used to his mechanical stride they went fast, for he was strong and resilient.

'Where are we running to?' he asked, seemingly not out of breath at all.

'Margate,' panted Jane, briefly pausing at a large signpost to check the direction. 'Margate,' she repeated grimly and broke into a run again.

They were walking down a long, wide, straight country road that carved its way through gentle hills. All the time Jane was trying to force herself to look back, for she was desperately afraid that Angel with his terrible smile would be walking softly behind them, gaining, gaining every moment. Several times she did glance round, but apart from the odd car there was no sign of anyone. Anyway, surely she would hear the roaring of an engine if Angel was after them, for he would be on his motor-bike.

Jane wondered if she was communicating her fears to Gary, but she was reassured to see him walking steadily on, his eyes fixed on the dark horizon, as if he was already seeing the winking, inviting lights of Margate.

Jane looked at her watch; it was well after ten and she was feeling utterly exhausted. Were they going to walk all night, she wondered. And how quickly would Gary find out that she didn't have the faintest idea where Margate was.

'It's quite a long way, isn't it?' he declared. 'Quite a long way to Margate.'

'We'll get there,' she said stubbornly.

'Yes.' He sounded quite confident. 'But it wasn't such a long way last time.'

'Last time?'

'When I ran home last time. It wasn't far at all.'

'That's because it was nearer,' said Jane sharply. 'Much nearer.'

'Isn't this nearer? This is nearer, isn't it?'

She wanted to scream aloud, to hit something – but not Gary. 'No, it's not nearer.'

'What's nearer?'

Of course, he probably had no sense of distance and perhaps not of time, so what did nearer really mean to him? Jane racked her brains and her exhaustion spread as she realized that the boy walking so tirelessly beside her lived in an inner world she could hardly penetrate. Yet the mystery of all this buoyed her up somehow and gave her extra strength, for however irritating Gary was, his mystery, to Jane at least, was not only a redeeming feature but also a particularly enthralling one.

An hour later she staggered and nearly fell but naturally Gary failed to notice. The road stretched on, rather like the road in the old-fashioned Start-Rite shoe advert, and bright moonlight illuminated its straight path. The hills still rose gently to left and right; the traffic had lessened and Gary didn't seem in the least tired, but Jane thought she would drop at any moment.

'I can see the sea,' said Gary expressionlessly.

'That's a patch of moonlight on the road.'

'I can see the sea,' stated Gary more loudly and more stubbornly and Jane felt that it was wise to say no more.

They were now in open countryside and the moon seemed brighter, harder. 'Boys and girls come out to play, the moon doth shine as bright as day.' The nursery rhyme beat in Jane's head until she could bear it no longer. The blood was pounding in her temples and her feet were leaden. A blister had appeared on her heel and every step was a relentless agony. Then she saw it, rising out of the flat countryside, almost obscured by an isolated copse of trees. The house was plain brick and had a blank, blind face. It was quite large and there was an ornate portico at the door and a scattering of outbuildings behind it. Even in the moonlight there was an atmosphere of desolation about the place. There were shutters at the windows, the gardens were completely overgrown and a couple of old abandoned cars were lying just inside the battered gates, one of which was off its hinges. But there was a light in the window by the door.

'You've stopped,' said Gary accusingly. 'You've stopped walking.' His voice was as hard and bright as the moon.

'I'm tired.'

'I'm not tired.'

'But I am. I'm going to knock at that door.' Jane looked at her watch. It was almost twelve and hardly a time to get anyone up, but she just couldn't go on and a chilly little wind had risen, convincing her that she would have no chance of getting any sleep in a hedgerow. Besides, she must phone Mrs Bird without Gary knowing; she hadn't felt she could simply walk into a telephone box with him beside her. She should phone her own parents too, because although she often stayed out late surely even they would begin to worry after twelve.

'Why are you going to knock at that door? What are you going to do it for?'

'See if we can sleep there.'

'No.'

'Gary – we won't make it to Margate if we're tired.'

'I'm not tired.'

The conversation was becoming circular. Then she heard the sound of the motor-bikes.

Chapter
Eleven

If they see us now, what will they do, wondered Jane desperately. She'd been sure all along they were there somewhere, searching for them, and somehow she knew that they always *would* be there. Maybe Ed would give up the chase eventually but she was certain that Angel wouldn't; she knew that he was dangerous and took a delight in hurting people.

'Come on.' She grabbed Gary's arm and he shook it off angrily. Too late she remembered how much he hated being touched.

'Let me go.'

'That boy's coming.'

'Who?'

'Angel – the one who hurt the old man.'

Gary nodded; he seemed to remember what had happened.

'He'll hurt us.'

'Why should he do that?'

Jane controlled herself with difficulty. 'Anyway, he'll stop us going to Margate. You'll never get to Dunroamin.'

There was a long silence while the roar of the motor-bikes grew louder and louder and Jane felt a surge of blind panic. She had never been in such a desperate plight in her life. Any moment now Angel would appear, Gary wouldn't budge – and they were standing outside a strange house which was either empty despite the light – or inhabited by someone who probably wouldn't let them in. All they could do was hide.

'All right,' said Gary. 'We'll have a quick sleep. What kind of bed will I be sleeping on? It won't have feathers, will it? They make me cough. And I want a hard pillow. My bed's got sides – in case I fall out. I like sides. Has this bed got sides?'

'Shut up.'

'What?'

'Shut up!'

It was too late. The motor-bikes were speeding up, and in the sharp moonlight Jane could see that Angel was smiling.

'Down.'

'Let go.'

Somehow she dragged him down into the ditch while to her horror the bikes came to a halt with a roar, their engines ticking over.

'I thought I saw something.' She could hear Ed's voice distinctly. 'Sure I did.'

'It's them all right. They must have come this way. That kid was determined to get to Margate, wasn't he?'

She had forgotten how silkily unpleasant Angel's voice was.

'Yeah, but I still don't see why we're after them.'

'You *know* why.'

'OK, they could identify us. But they're only kids –
and one of 'em wasn't even all there.'

'So what. They can still recognize us.' Angel
laughed gently.

'What are we going to do?' Ed's voice quavered
and Jane knew he was feeling well out of his depth.

'We're going to put the fear of God into them,' said
Angel. 'They won't grass us up after I've finished
with them.'

'But what are you going to *do*?' insisted Ed fearfully.

'Shh.'

'Eh?'

'Thought I heard something.'

Gary had shifted and Jane put a cautioning finger
to her lips. But he wasn't taking any notice; instead he
was beginning to pile up some sticks into a miniature
pyramid.

'Do you think they've gone in there?' asked Ed.

'The house? That's Mrs Lamb's place.'

'Isn't she a hermit?'

'Another nutter,' said Angel softly. Then he added,
'That gives me an idea.'

'What idea?' asked Ed reluctantly.

'Old Parkinson, Mrs Lamb – they're weirdos, aren't
they? Live in their own little worlds right away from
anyone else.' Angel's voice was calculating.

'So what if they do?'

'And they keep their money close to them, don't
they?'

There was a long pause. 'What are you on about?'
said Ed at last, his voice rising in panic.

'Suppose we had four grand – five grand – not just
a crummy two.'

54

'It's enough.'

'What for? We'll soon get through it.' Angel's voice was insistent now. 'With a bit more we can go abroad – down to the South of France, Ed.'

'No way.'

'But there must *be* a way, Ed. There *must* be.'

'Why?'

'Because we killed the old man.'

'No we didn't.'

'But we did. You didn't hear him breathing, did you, Ed? He's a goner, isn't he? And you know what that means. You know what that means, don't you, Ed?'

'Yeah.'

'We're going to be nicked if we stay here. We've got to get away. Abroad. We could do life.'

Gary continued to build his miniature pyramid of sticks and pushed Jane's hand away when she tried to stop him.

'So you're saying we should kill Mrs Wotsit too?' asked Ed incredulously.

'Parkinson was an accident.'

'So –'

'We've got to break in and take a look.'

'If we're caught –'

'We won't be.'

'Suppose those kids are in there?'

'With her? She wouldn't let anyone in.'

'So –' Ed stuttered. 'You say we're going in now.'

'Not now. It's too early. She might be up. Besides – I'm starved.'

'So am I.' Ed seemed to cheer up now that food had been mentioned and the break-in put off – albeit temporarily.

'We'll go to that all-night transport café over by Cams Common.'

'Great.'

'Then we'll come back.'

'But –'

'I said we'd come back, Ed.' Angel's voice was steely.

'OK. What about those kids then?'

'We'd better take a look.'

'I swore I heard something,' said Ed with conviction.

'We'll take a look in the woods,' replied Angel gently. 'If not, they could be in the house. Yeah?'

'Maybe.'

'And they can wait for a bit if they are.'

A car cruised by as Angel and Ed pulled their bikes on to the side of the road and dismounted. This was it, thought Jane, the panic surging through her again. She felt as if she was going to be sick at any moment, particularly when Gary gave a grunt of satisfaction as his pyramid rose a little higher.

Jane froze as Angel and Ed clumped through the undergrowth.

'Where did you hear the noise?' she heard Angel say.

'Up that path,' Ed stage-whispered. 'Follow it and see if they're hiding. I'll try this way.'

'OK.' Angel sounded annoyed, as if he didn't like taking orders from Ed of all people, but he walked on and disappeared up the path. As soon as he'd vanished, to Jane's absolute horror, Ed began to walk swiftly and determinedly towards them.

*

Again she froze rigid, hardly daring to breathe, and noting with tremendous relief that Gary had come to an intricate part of his building programme and, tongue slightly protruding, was silently placing stick after stick on a fragile and slightly tottering pile. She prayed he would stay quiet, that the pile of twigs would not suddenly crash down, making Gary give an angry outburst, but still Ed moved towards them with such precision that she was convinced he knew where they were.

'Psst.'

Jane said nothing, holding her breath, the sweat running down her forehead.

'Psst.'

Oh God – Gary was looking up.

'Yes?' he said in his clear, monotonous voice.

'Shh,' Ed replied urgently and suddenly Jane felt very confused.

'Do you know the way to Margate?' asked Gary brightly, not in the least anxious to be quiet.

'Shut up!' hissed Ed and Jane in an unlikely Greek chorus.

'I've only got a minute,' whispered Ed.

'Do you know –' Gary began to repeat.

'Shut him up somehow, can't you?' Ed pleaded and Jane, still utterly bewildered and at a complete loss to understand the situation, was seized with desperate inspiration and said to Gary, 'He'll tell us if you keep quiet.'

Gary nodded and waited, ominously patient.

'Is he –' Ed began but Jane interrupted ruthlessly.

'What do you want?'

'To warn you. Stay where you are and I'll try to steer him away.'

Suddenly Jane realized that Ed was as terrified of Angel as she was. 'Thanks,' she gasped at him.

'In these moods, he's a right – anyway, he's dangerous, right?'

'Yes.'

'Don't move an inch.'

'Do you know the way to –' began Gary.

'Tell him.' Jane had total eye contact with Ed, and somehow she was able to convince him more with that look than with anything she could ever have tried to explain to him in words.

'To where?' whispered Ed.

'Margate,' said Gary.

'Shh. Yeah – you're heading the right way. Just keep on down the road. It's quite a walk.'

'We're going to stay in a house. That house. Jane's tired,' Gary announced.

Again Ed's and Jane's eyes met.

'I heard all you said,' Jane stated bleakly.

'Oh yes?'

'We're still going to stay there.' She only made up her mind as she said the words, but as she spoke Jane knew she had no other course of action. Not now. Not with what she knew. 'We're going to stay there and I'm going to ring the police and get them to come out and –'

'Only one drawback to that,' said Ed. 'I know for a fact Mrs Lamb doesn't have a phone.'

'Mrs Lamb doesn't have a phone,' chanted Gary.

Ed was moving away. 'Don't go there,' he said. 'Angel's going to break in.'

'I know,' said Jane fiercely. 'I'll be telling that to Mrs Lamb.'

'I couldn't see anyone up there,' said Angel's voice.

Jane could hear Ed's footsteps moving away from them.

'What about you?'

'Nothing,' replied Ed. 'Not a sign of anybody. I must have heard an animal scuttling about or something.'

'Wonder if they *are* in that house?'

'Come on,' said Ed. 'Let's go. They could be further down the road. Anyway I'm starving.'

'All right, Ed.' Angel's voice was silky smooth. 'But I'm not playing games. We'll be back to call on Mrs Lamb.'

'We'd be fools,' replied Ed grimly. 'The police will be looking for us; we should be putting distance between us and them. The old girl probably hasn't got a bean.'

'We'll see about that,' said Angel.

There was a long silence during which Gary, contented by the information he had received about Margate, still continued to build his pyramid of twigs.

Chapter
Twelve

For a few more seconds Jane lay there, weighing up the consequences of what she was going to do while Ed and Angel revved up and took off on their motor-cycles. Why didn't she just walk on with Gary, make the excuse that she should have done earlier, go into the telephone box and then be confident that someone would pick them up. Surely she could fool Gary fairly easily providing he was given some reasonable re-assurances.

The alternative seemed pure folly: to invade the house of an old and possibly eccentric recluse and give her some garbled story of a burglary to come. She probably wouldn't believe a word she said. And what about Gary? Surely Mrs Lamb would find him so strange that she would never listen to anything she had to say. Gary would want to know if she knew the way to Margate – and she definitely wouldn't say the right things to him. And Jane knew she certainly couldn't rely on Ed to restrain Angel; he was obviously as frightened of him as she was. Only Gary remained oblivious of any danger, and in a way she found relief in his single-minded obsessiveness. If only she too simply had to worry about getting to Margate. But despite all the difficulties, Jane knew that she couldn't possibly leave the unfortunate Mrs Lamb to her fate. Hadn't the death of the old café owner been enough? She had to protect her – no matter what the odds.

'We're going in,' said Jane to Gary, 'only for a quick sleep.' But she knew that sleep was very far from her mind now. All she wanted to do was to warn the old lady and then head for a telephone box. Surely that would be possible. She looked at Gary with sudden renewed affection. He had his own way of doing things, but they weren't going to be of much help to her.

'We're going to the house, are we?'

'Yes.'

'I hope she's got the right kind of bed. I can't sleep on feathers – and I've got to have a hard pillow and –' Gary went on reciting his litany as they crossed the road to the neglected, blank-eyed house. 'There's a lot of rubbish around,' he commented disapprovingly.

'It'll be better inside,' replied Jane without much hope as she rang the bell. Surprisingly, it worked, and she heard its jangling echo reverberating around the interior. For a long while nothing happened and she tried again.

'Are you sure this house is occupied?' asked Gary demandingly.

'She'll come.'

But no one came. Jane was about to ring the bell for a third time when she heard something. Could it be shuffling steps in hastily drawn-on carpet slippers, or was it just her imagination? Then Jane knew she was right as a whole series of bolts began to be drawn back – a process which seemed to take ages.

Eventually the door swung open, still secured by a chain.

'What do you want?' the voice rasped as if it was not used very often, and Jane found it impossible to guess the age of the speaker.

'I've got to speak to you, Mrs Lamb.'

'How do you know my name?'

'I was told.'

'By whom?' She sounded very formal and Gary moved restlessly from one foot to the other.

'It was mentioned by someone who's going to burgle your house,' said Jane, and then realized how ridiculous she must sound.

'Have you woken me up to deride me, child?' The rasping sound grew thinner.

'No, it's the truth. They said you were old and –'

'Who are you?'

'Jane Lomax. And this is Gary Bird – my friend.'

'Good evening,' said Gary formally. 'I do hope you're not expecting me to sleep on feathers.'

'You're talking in riddles,' snapped Mrs Lamb. 'What's all this about feathers and burglars?'

Jane felt the situation was getting quite beyond her but she was determined to persevere. 'Please let us in. We don't mean you any harm. Or phone the police if you want –'

'I don't have a phone.'

'Then let me phone for you.'

'That boy – this boy Gary. Who is he?'

'I'm Gary Bird. I live at 14 Birch Drive, Bell Farm Estate. My telephone number is Dixbury 491463.'

There was a long, surprised silence, then the voice said, 'I'm letting you in. I know I shouldn't, but it's all so odd that I can't imagine you're lying. Be careful, though — I've got a curtain rod in my hand and I'm not as old and defenceless as you think.'

'What have you got a curtain rod in your hand for?' asked Gary brightly.

Without replying, Mrs Lamb unhooked the security chain and the door swung open.

Chapter
Thirteen

The hall was lit with a pale, naked bulb, and while it was certainly true that Mrs Lamb was not as old as Jane had originally thought, she was certainly incredibly strange. Mrs Lamb could not have been more than fifty and she was enormously fat. Her hair, which was soft and golden, tumbled about her shoulders and down to her waist. She wore a long black dress with an old dressing-gown thrown over the top. Her smooth, round features were quiet and kind-looking and her eyes were a light, compelling green. In her hair she had pinned a very large tortoiseshell clip and on her feet she wore a pair of black shoes with silver buckles that shone in the pale light.

'This doesn't look very comfortable, does it?' said Gary bluntly, staring round the bare hall, and Jane closed her eyes in embarrassment. When she opened them again, she could see that Mrs Lamb was smiling, her features almost dissolving into the fatty folds of her face. She had a large number of wobbling, juddering chins but her fleshy smile was one of the nicest Jane had ever seen.

'I only live in one room,' said Mrs Lamb. 'The house is too big for me.' She seemed to be directly addressing Gary, with only a glance or two in Jane's direction. It seemed as if she understood Gary quite naturally and immediately. 'Would you like to come and see it?'

'As long as you don't have a feather bed.'

'Mine's rock hard. I can't bear feathers.'

'I don't like them either,' said Gary. He looked at Mrs Lamb's hands. 'Where is your curtain rod?'

'I'm afraid that was a little white lie.'

Gary stared at her and repeated, 'A little white lie.' Jane knew that he couldn't understand what she meant but she also knew that Mrs Lamb realized that too.

'Come and see my room.' She turned away and led them down a long corridor. Then she opened a door on to a truly remarkable sight. Inside the large shuttered drawing-room was the most amazing clutter of things that Jane had ever seen. In the centre was a huge four-poster bed with a torn canopy over it. On the floor, piled on chairs and tables, overflowing on to a sideboard, stacked in corners, heaped in tottering piles, were hundreds and hundreds and hundreds of books. They filled the room completely except for an area by the shuttered French windows. There stood a doll's-house, but not an ordinary doll's-house; it was enormous, so big you could get inside it with the beautiful little dolls.

'It's the way I live,' said Mrs Lamb. 'I don't need anyone or anything else. No one usually comes in – not if I can help it – but you're only kids and you had a pretty weird story.'

'What's that Dunroamin?' asked Gary.

'Dunroamin?'

'He means the doll's-house,' explained Jane.

'It's the only family heirloom I kept. We've lived in this house for centuries, my family.' She paused. 'But when my beloved husband was taken from me so many years ago I sold everything and moved in here.' She looked round. 'Jack and I were very fond of books – we used to read to each other – and if I keep on reading I can hear his voice. I've been doing that for a very long time now.' Her voice tailed away as she watched Gary staring at the doll's-house, utterly captivated.

'May I go inside?' he asked. 'May I go inside? Am I allowed to do that?'

'Of course you are,' said Mrs Lamb. 'Now, child,' she said, turning to Jane, 'what is this extraordinary story you were going to tell me?'

Jane explained everything from her original meeting with Gary, his obsessive activities, his running away from home and the horrendous scene outside the little café in the park. Then she went on to tell her about the other events that had led her to come and warn Mrs Lamb about Angel – and the unwilling, dominated, frightened Ed. 'Do you believe me?' she asked eagerly. 'You *must* believe me.'

'Yes, I believe you. It's too strange a story not to. He's quite a person, isn't he, your Gary? I wonder if he's capable of love?'

'I don't know,' said Jane. 'He just lives in his own world.' She told her all over again about the spinning and the barrel and the building and Dunroamin.

When she had finished, Mrs Lamb nodded. 'I understand,' she said. 'It's security, I suppose. Looks as if he's found some already.'

Jane turned and was startled to see that Gary was sitting in the hallway of the doll's-house. It was small and its walls totally enclosed him so that he was a very tight fit indeed. Already his head was nodding and his eyes closing.

'I understand him,' said Mrs Lamb. 'I feel much the same.' She looked across at her piles of books. 'I've got my routine – my obsession. I couldn't be without it.'

Jane nodded, not wanting to bring her back to the matter in hand too abruptly, but knowing that she had to soon. Time was passing far too quickly.

'We should get to a telephone box,' Jane told her. She looked at her watch. It was almost two o'clock in the morning but she had never felt more wide awake. 'We're in danger here. We've got to alert the police. They're already looking for those two.'

'I've got a car,' said Mrs Lamb surprisingly.

'What?' Jane was amazed.

'Well, I've got to eat, haven't I? I've got to go shopping. Or do you think I eat books?' She laughed suddenly and it was rich, deep and infectious. 'I may be a funny old recluse but I actually do go to Tesco's. I'll get the keys and we'll ring the police and reassure both your parents and Gary's mother. Then we'll come back, have a rest and if his mother gives her permission, I'll drive Gary to Margate – just for a visit.'

'What?' Jane was flabbergasted by all the solutions.

'Well, it's not that far and contrary to what you think I can just fit behind the wheel – and I like to think I'm a pretty efficient driver.'

'I didn't mean –'

'I know you didn't. I'll get my keys now and try to

tempt Gary out of the doll's-house. I think he'll come when he knows where he's going – eventually. Why don't you go to the front door and peer out very carefully and see if the coast is clear.'

Jane could have hugged Mrs Lamb's ample frame. Instead she said, 'You've just taken a real load off my mind.'

'I haven't done that for anybody for a very long time,' Mrs Lamb replied with a sigh.

Jane walked down the bare corridor to the equally bare hallway and paused by the front door. It took some time to understand how it should be unbolted but soon she was down to the chain. Gently slipping it off, very slowly and cautiously she opened the door, but before she had moved it only a couple of centimetres it was kicked wide open and the force knocked Jane flying back into the hallway. On the threshold stood Angel. He was alone and he was smiling.

Chapter
Fourteen

'Don't shout out,' he said very gently. 'If you do, I'll kill you.' As if in a slow-motion dream, Jane saw him pull the long thin knife out of his belt. She lay on the floor, looking up at him, knowing without a shadow of doubt that he didn't care about anyone.

'Where's Ed?' she whispered.

'He's chickened out. I expect the police have caught him by now.'

'Did you do something to him?'

Angel's smile broadened as he fingered the knife. 'Now what would *I* have done to Ed?'

He could have done anything to him, she thought – like he would do anything to her – to them. In her mind's eye Jane saw Gary, secure in his doll's-house, Mrs Lamb looking for the car keys – all her problems over.

Angel's voice broke into her thoughts. 'Get up,' he whispered.

Slowly she rose to her feet, her back against the cold wall.

'Don't say a word.'

'What are you going to do?'

'I'm going to see if the old lady has any money, aren't I?'

'You won't hurt her –'

He stepped nearer, the knife in his hand, the long, thin blade pointing at her stomach. 'Not her.'

'What do you mean by that?'

'You and your friend. You know what I look like, don't you?' He pulled a balaclava from his pocket and slipped it over his head. 'But the old lady won't, will she?'

'I didn't think you'd care whether you hurt her or not,' Jane blurted out, aghast at the aggression of her words. She watched the smile disappear from Angel's face.

'She could be my mother,' he said, and his voice shook.

'So you'd rob your own mother?' Again she was amazed at the way she was talking to him. Perhaps she was so desperate she didn't really care. The smile did not return to Angel's face and, instead, his lip curled in a snarl of rage, but it was much less frightening than his smile, for at least the rage made him human.

'Shut up!'

'And I don't know why you're so worried about us seeing you – not if you're going to the South of France.'

'So you were there. You *were* listening. I said that when we stopped in the woods. When we started searching for you.'

'Yes. We were there. Hiding.'

'Did Ed know that?' he whispered menacingly, still exhibiting his little boy temper, but even so she wasn't afraid.

'No. We were in the ditch – and we listened to both of you.'

Without warning the smile suddenly returned to Angel's face and Jane was afraid all over again.

'He made me walk up that path.'

'He didn't know we were there,' insisted Jane.

The smile intensified. 'I think you're telling a porky, aren't you?' The knife came nearer. 'Now lead on, little girl.'

'Where?'

'To the others, of course. And you know what will happen if you shout out, don't you?'

'I don't –'

'I'll stick you, my darling. So help me God, I'll stick you.'

Jane walked on down the corridor towards the light with Angel only a few centimetres behind her. She could hear him breathing and smell some kind of cologne he was wearing. It smelt of tangy pine but it only made her want to be sick. She longed to shout out but she also knew that he meant what he said, and every time she tried to warn Mrs Lamb and Gary, something stuck horribly in her throat and nothing came out.

Soon she was walking into the extraordinary room. Mrs Lamb had her back to her and she was bending over, displaying a vast black bottom, talking to Gary.

'I want you to come out now.' There was a note of impatience in her voice.

'I'm afraid I'm waiting for my friend,' came Gary's monotone.

'She'll be back in a minute. We're all going to Margate.'

'I'm afraid I'll have to wait for my friend first.'

Jane was very moved as she heard Gary's trusting comments. Could she have actually partly superseded Margate, or had she become an essential travelling companion? Could it really be true that Gary wouldn't go to Margate without her? If it was true it was incredible.

Gary's dependence on her gave Jane the strength to shout out, 'He's here! Angel's here!'

She felt a sharp blow to the side of her head and reeled forward, just managing to keep on her feet.

'Don't move, anybody.'

Mrs Lamb turned round ponderously. 'Oh dear,' she said inadequately.

Gary emerged slowly from the doll's-house and looked up at Angel trustingly. 'Could I ride on your motor-bike?' he asked. 'Wouldn't that be quicker?' He gazed round at them all. 'Wouldn't that be a quicker way to Margate?'

Chapter
Fifteen

'Shut up!'

Gary stared at Angel blankly. 'You shouldn't play with knives,' he said reprovingly.

'If someone doesn't shut that weird kid up, I'll do him.'

'It's all right, Gary,' gasped Jane. 'We'll be on the road again soon.'

'On that motor-bike?'

'Maybe.'

Gary was silent, standing by the doll's-house, temporarily satisfied by the arrangement, but Jane knew he wouldn't be for long and she had a sudden idea.

'Why don't you build something while you're waiting? You could use the books, couldn't he?' She turned in desperation to Mrs Lamb.

'Of course he can,' she replied.

Gary nodded and slowly began to pile up the books.

For a few seconds Angel watched him and then he turned to Mrs Lamb.

'Don't waste my time, lady. Give it to me.'

'What do you want?' Her voice was very calm.

'The money you keep here.'

'I keep all my money in the bank.'

Angel grabbed Jane and pulled her to him, placing the knife at her throat.

'I'm going to kill her,' he said, 'unless you give me the money.'

Jane knew he meant what he said.

So did Mrs Lamb. She stood a little in front of Gary who, after an initial stare at Angel, resumed piling his books up, carefully choosing the flattest and the widest as a base.

'Very well,' she said. 'You can have what I've got.'

'I want everything.'

'You can have what I've got.' She went to pull something from under the bed, tugging away without much effect. 'You'll have to help me,' she said.

'You go,' said Angel, pushing at Jane.

'No. 'Mrs Lamb was insistent.'A child can't shift this.'

'OK. You stay where you are,' Angel said to Jane. 'Try anything and I'll stick the old lady.'

'Not so old,' puffed Mrs Lamb. 'I'm only just fifty.'

Angel grabbed at the handle of the trunk and they both pulled. It came forward a couple of centimetres.

'Let's change sides,' she said. 'It'll be easier that way.'

'I can't see why,' Angel grumbled. 'It's coming, isn't it?'

'Either you want the money or you don't,' Mrs Lamb stated flatly as she stepped past him.

'How do you get it out on your own?' Angel went on grumbling and Jane noticed how young he suddenly sounded, as if he was just a sulky kid. How old was he anyway? He probably wasn't much more than seventeen or so, but he had the knife tucked into his belt and Jane knew that he would be very quick to pull it out.

'Come on,' said Angel. 'I haven't got all night.'

Mrs Lamb picked up the china vase from the bedside table so quickly that Jane was amazed by her dexterity. She brought it down on Angel's head with stunning force.

He gave a little whimper, tried to stand up and keeled over backwards, striking his head again on the threadbare carpet.

'Good gracious,' said Mrs Lamb. 'I was never a woman of action. I've just read about this kind of thing in books.'

'Well, you've gone and done it now,' said Jane, taking a tentative look at the prostrate Angel. There was a patch of dark blood on his hairline and a trickle of it was seeping down his forehead.

'He's all right,' said Mrs Lamb with flustered confidence. She felt his pulse. 'Well, this is beating very strongly.'

'What are we going to do?' asked Jane, the shock waves leaping about inside her. She felt sick again and, above all, utterly exhausted and indecisive.

'Tie him up. Where's his friend?'

'He said he'd chickened out.'

'That's all right then.' She looked around her. 'I had a tow rope for the car here once –'

'It needs towing?'

'She used to. Jack used to get her going by pulling her with a tractor, but she's got a new engine now.'

'Wouldn't you keep a tow rope in the garage?'

'No,' said Mrs Lamb sharply. 'It was Jack's. Everything of Jack's is in this room.' She knelt down by the bed again and pulled out a long, thick rope. 'Know anything about knots?' she asked.

Gary had already built his books to a considerable height and went on building them as they clumsily tied Angel's hands and feet. It was difficult with one rope – Jane didn't know anything about knots at all and neither did Mrs Lamb. In the end, however, they succeeded in trussing him up and as they stood back panting to study their handiwork, Gary looked across from his book skyscraper and said, 'Is that a good game?'

'It's Angel,' said Jane. 'He was going to stop us going to Margate. Mrs Lamb knocked him out and we tied him up.'

'He's hurt.' Gary stood up and showed emotion for the first time. 'He's bloody. I don't like bloody.'

'He'll be all right,' said Jane soothingly.

'No.' He was defying her now and she could see that he was working himself up into a tantrum just as he had done when they had fought in the street. He went to his pile of books and kicked them over.

'No.' he yelled. 'No – no – no – no. Don't like bloody. Won't have bloody.' Gary kicked at more books. Angel opened his eyes and groaned and Mrs Lamb walked across to Gary.

'Don't kick Jack's books,' she said.

Gary kicked another and for a moment Jane thought Mrs Lamb was going to lose control and hit him. If she did, Jane was sure this would provoke a worse

76

tantrum. Maybe Gary was just tired, maybe he was really horrified by the blood – either way he was well out of control.

In the end Mrs Lamb regained her own control and said quietly to Gary, whose face was screwed up with fear and rage, 'It's off to Margate now.'

'Dunroamin!' yelled Gary.

'You bet. Dunroamin it is.' She looked at her watch. 'You'll be there by morning.'

'Bloody!'

'Tell you what – go in the doll's-house for a bit.'

'Bloody!'

'There it is.'

Gary reluctantly turned round, his shoulders rigid, and looked suspiciously at the doll's-house. Then Jane saw his shoulders droop and relax and he crammed himself inside the minute hallway, the sturdy wood embracing and holding him in a tight wedged grip. He visibly relaxed all over and his eyelids fluttered and then closed.

'You'll pay,' whispered Angel. His face was paler than ever but the blood was drying on his forehead. 'You'll pay – and go on paying.'

'Absolute nonsense,' said Mrs Lamb briskly. 'The police will be here soon.'

'You're not on the phone,' he sneered.

'No, but I have a car, and we're going to ring them.'

'What about Gary?' asked Jane. 'We can't leave him here alone with – with him.'

'I'll go.'

'Suppose your car won't start?' Jane was panicking now as her one figure of security prepared to leave.

'She will – I had her out this morning. Don't worry – I'll be ten minutes. A quarter of an hour at the outside. Then as soon as we can coax Gary out we'll all set out for the calls to your parents and a trip to Margate.' She sounded brisk and authoritative.

'All right,' said Jane reluctantly.

Mrs Lamb bent her massive bulk over the trussed-up Angel and checked his bonds. 'They're fine,' she said.

He spat at her and she ducked too late. Wiping the spittle off her cheek Mrs Lamb calmly passed Jane another vase. 'If he gives you any trouble, hit him with this,' she said briskly. 'It's of no value and neither of them belonged to Jack. They both belonged to Mother and we never got on. I don't know why I kept them.' Rattling her car keys, Mrs Lamb abruptly left the room. 'I shan't be long,' she called, leaving Jane and Angel uneasily contemplating each other.

'You'll pay,' whispered Angel.

'Shut up,' said Jane, summoning up all her courage.

'The bogeyman's coming,' said Gary loudly but sleepily. Jane realized he was dreaming and Angel gave her a pallid smile.

For at least a couple of minutes Jane and Angel tried to stare each other out. His eyes were gleaming maliciously and the gentle, uncaring smile that had so terrified her was back on his lips. Then, suddenly, it faded and was replaced by a look of intense suffering.

'My head –'

'What is it?'

'It hurts so badly. You've got to help me.'

'Mrs Lamb has gone to get help,' said Jane very coldly. 'She won't be long.'

'I need an ambulance.'

'You'll get the police.'

'Supposing I die? What would you do then?' he said, his sulky little boyishness becoming more evident. 'You'd be a murderer,' he whispered. 'Have you thought about that?'

'Like you,' replied Jane.

'The bogeyman's coming,' repeated Gary in his sleep.

'He is and all,' replied Angel, that terrible smile returning to his face.

Chapter
Sixteen

What was that she heard in the corridor – a footstep? Angel's smile widened. Of course, thought Jane with relief, it must be Mrs Lamb. She looked at her watch. Bit early, wasn't it? She'd only been gone five minutes. Maybe she'd come back for something.

'Mrs Lamb?' Jane cried out. 'Mrs Lamb?'

There was no reply at all but she could have sworn she heard another footstep.

'The bogeyman's coming,' chuckled Angel.

'Shut up.'

'But he *is*.'

That was another footstep – she was absolutely sure of it. 'Who's there? Mrs Lamb, is that you? Is that you?'

There was no reply.

Jane could bear it no longer. Trembling all over, evading Angel's mocking eyes, she hurried out to stare down the corridor. There was no one there at all. Deciding that it must be a trick of her imagination, she returned to the room, marched past Angel and sat on Mrs Lamb's bed with her back to him, but straining her ears.

She was absolutely certain there was another footstep – and then another.

'Bogeyman,' whispered Angel. 'Bogeyman.'

'Oh, shut up.'

'He's *coming*!'

Jane sat rigidly with her back to the door, tensed as she had never been tensed before. She kept hearing footsteps now and she couldn't work out whether they were real or not.

'He's *coming*!' purred Angel.

'Shut up!' She went to the door again and looked out while Angel chuckled in a horrible, gloating way which soon became an awful convulsive giggling. There was no one out there and she banged the door to, determined that this would block off the nightmarish fantasies – if they were fantasies.

'Shut up!' She could have smashed the other china vase over his big head there and then as the uncontrollable giggling continued, but she knew she couldn't really. Gradually his giggling subsided as she sat again on the bed with her back to him, watching Gary sleeping so securely, so rigidly, in his doll's-house hallway – a temporary Dunroamin – knowing how deeply fond of him she had become. There was something immensely reassuring to his pattern of life, to his tunnel vision, his obsessions, his single-mindedness, his repetitiveness. Jane felt she could understand him, relate to him, find kinship with him.

Suddenly the door began to creak, and when she whipped round she saw that it was slowly opening.

Ed stood on the threshold, grinning. 'You play games with us,' he said. 'I'll play games with you.'

'What – what are you doing here?' She was utterly bewildered and temporarily numb.

'I'm with Angel.' His look changed. 'What have you done to him?'

'They'll pay, Ed. They'll pay.' Angel's smile was the worst, the most threatening she had ever, ever seen.

'He said you'd gone.'

'He was lying, wasn't he?' grinned Ed. 'I was on watch. But when nothing happened for so long I moved in.'

'Ed had a little confession to make,' said Angel gently. 'But he's forgiven now.'

'Forgiven. Forgiven for what?'

'For protecting you,' replied Angel. 'In the end he had to tell me you were hiding in that ditch – and he knew it.'

'He only told you,' said Jane, 'because he's scared of you.'

'Me?' said Ed and he laughed uneasily.

'Get these ropes off,' snapped Angel. 'The old lady's gone for the police.'

'No she ain't.'

'What?'

'I saw her going to the garage, so I clobbered her, didn't I?' Ed looked across at Angel for approval and Jane's heart gave a sudden lurch.

'Did you?' Jane asked, willing him to deny it.

'Yeah.'

'And you're going to untie that – thing – when you know how dangerous he is?'

'Yeah.'

'You can't. He'll kill us all.' Jane was so terrified now that she felt completely numb.

'He's my mate.'

'You're just scared of him.'

There was a long, long pause during which Jane became more and more convinced, on no evidence at all, that Ed had *not* 'clobbered' Mrs Lamb. She didn't know exactly what it was, possibly there was something about his eyes – something about the shifty look in them – that convinced her. Had he seen her go – let her go – yet wanted to give Angel a chance? She was sure that this was the case and now he was wondering what on earth he should do.

'Come on,' snapped Angel with a new edge to his voice. 'Get moving, Ed.'

'All right.'

'If you untie him,' repeated Jane, 'he'll kill us all. Come on, admit it – you let Mrs Lamb drive off in the car. You know she's safe – you know the police will be here any minute. If you untie him you'll be in worse trouble than ever.'

Ed hesitated and for the first time, with a kind of manic glee, Jane knew from the look on Angel's face that he, too, was having doubts.

'Ed!'

'Wait a minute.'

'What do you mean – wait a minute?' Angel was livid, but he was also beginning to look afraid.

'I'll do it.' Ed stood there, doing nothing.

'Now!'

'Yeah.'

'Now, Ed.'

'No!' Jane yelled, waking up Gary who yawned and stretched and began to crawl out of the hallway of the doll's-house.

'Hallo,' he said, looking up at the dithering Ed. 'Do you know the way to Margate?'

Chapter
Seventeen

'Shut that damned kid up,' growled Angel. 'Shut him up now.'

'Don't worry,' said Jane as steadily as she could, 'Mrs Lamb's gone to get the car.'

'It's taking an awful long *time* to get to Margate,' complained Gary, stretching again.

'We'll be there by morning,' replied Jane comfortingly.

'Get me untied, Ed. Now!' yelled Angel in a high-pitched, uncontrolled voice. It sounded to Jane as if he was going to burst into hysterical tears at any moment.

'All right.' Ed began to walk towards him.

'Ed!' It was Jane's turn to yell. 'Don't do it.'

But she knew instinctively that she had lost.

Slowly but very surely, Ed began to untie Angel's bonds.

'You don't know what you're doing,' said Jane, trying to appear calm for Gary's sake.

'Are they *all* coming to Margate?' asked Gary. He stared at them thoughtfully. 'It's going to be crowded in Mrs Lamb's car. Maybe Mrs Lamb has a big car.

Some people have big cars, don't they, Jane? Has Mrs Lamb got a big car?' He was obviously becoming very anxious.

'Yes,' said Jane as soothingly as she could. 'She does have a big car.'

'*Shut that kid up!*' Angel was beside himself, gritting his teeth, his voice still high and emotional.

'He can't help it,' replied Ed.

'I'll kill him.'

Ed stopped untying the rope. 'What?'

'I'll kill him.'

'He's got a knife,' said Jane. 'It fell on the floor – over there.' Both she and Mrs Lamb had forgotten to pick it up.

Ed paused. 'I haven't seen that before,' he said slowly.

'I had it as a kid.' Angel's voice was more reasonable, almost wheedling now.

'It's lethal.'

'You don't think I'd use it, do you?'

'I don't know. You've already –'

'Shut up,' yelled Angel. 'Shut up about that.'

'I don't like shouting,' said Gary. 'You mustn't shout if you're coming in Mrs Lamb's car.'

'He won't,' said Jane. She was very conscious of Gary's anxiety now and was afraid that he would fall into a tantrum which wouldn't help the situation one little bit.

'I hope not,' said Gary reprovingly. 'I don't like shouting.'

'Come on, finish the job, Ed.' The wheedling note was back in Angel's voice.

'OK.'

'And leave the knife where it is,' he added.

Jane felt a surge of panic run right through her as Angel stood up. He was eyeing her almost greedily, as if he was relishing the chance to do her damage, but directly he moved a few paces forward, he swayed and nearly collapsed. Ed rapidly picked up the knife and almost simultaneously grabbed him.

'It's my head,' Angel said, giving Jane a vicious look. 'It's killing me.' He gazed at the knife in Ed's hand. 'Give me that.' With a sigh Ed passed it over to him and Angel stared at him searchingly. 'Did you let her go or not?'

Ed said nothing.

'I have to know.'

Still Ed said nothing.

'Please.'

'OK.' Ed's voice was abrupt. 'I let her go.'

'You idiot.'

'I couldn't hurt her. Couldn't see any more people get hurt.'

'People mustn't get hurt,' stated Gary, and for a moment Jane was afraid that Angel was going to turn on him in earnest, but he was too distracted by Ed's admission.

'You idiot,' he repeated.

Ed shrugged.

'We've got seconds,' spat out Angel. 'Just seconds. Give me a hand with this thing under the bed.'

'What thing?' asked Ed in surprise.

'It's got money in, stupid. Come on.' Angel lurched towards the bed with his face paler than ever and the sweat dripping down his brow. Ed knelt beside him and together they hauled out the large and dusty trunk.

'We'll have to break it open,' said Angel, but now his voice was thin and indistinct.

'Let's see.' Ed fiddled with the catches and the lid sprang up. Inside it was full of books.

'Are you taking those to Margate?' asked Gary, coming over to have a look and suicidally addressing Angel. 'Are you a great reader?'

Angel said nothing.

'Do you like reading those books?'

Still Angel said nothing.

'I like reading picture books. Do you like picture books? Are you taking picture books to Margate? Are those books picture books? Can I have a look at the picture books? I didn't find any picture books before. Unfortunately.'

Angel got up and slapped Gary around the face.

It was a stinging blow and Gary rocked back on his heels. There was a short silence while everyone watched Gary's colour change to brick red. With an angry roar he charged at Angel and head-butted him in the stomach. Angel went down and Gary jumped on him, fists flailing. Trying to protect his injured head Angel rolled over – and Gary rolled over with him, punching and kicking as hard as he could. Then Jane saw Angel's hand reaching for the knife that he had tucked into his belt.

'Ed,' she screamed. 'Stop him. He'll kill Gary.'

But the knife had already clattered to the floor again as the combatants rolled about amongst the books.

*

The police siren shrilled outside as Mrs Lamb's bulky figure appeared in the doorway.

'Get him off!' screeched Angel, pinned helplessly to the floor.

'Who are you?' said Mrs Lamb to Ed.

'I'm Ed.'

'What are you doing in my house?'

'Er –'

'Get him off!' screamed Angel again.

'Gary, leave him,' yelled Jane. It was like calling off a dog – and a very disobedient dog at that. For the next few seconds Gary continued to rain blows and kicks on the struggling, wounded Angel, and then he suddenly became aware of the sirens and stood up panting.

'It's the police,' he said, turning to Jane. 'Can I have a ride in their car?'

'It's all up, Angel,' said Ed hopelessly.

'No it's not.' Battered, bleeding, staggering, swaying, Angel was nevertheless on his feet and again he had the long, thin knife in his hand.

With amazing speed, Angel had grabbed Jane and held the knife to her throat. He dragged her to him, putting an arm round her neck.

'It's never all up,' he snarled to Ed. 'Not when you've got a hostage anyway.' Angel turned Jane and himself towards Mrs Lamb. 'Where *is* the money?' he said more calmly.

'I don't –'

'But you do. I'll kill her. I've got nothing to lose now.'

'Pack it in, Angel,' advised Ed. 'It'll go better if you do.'

But Angel ignored him. 'Where is it?'

'I don't have much.'

'How much?'

'Five hundred.'

'You're lying.'

'I'm *not*.'

The desperation in Mrs Lamb's voice only confirmed his suspicion that she was holding out on him. 'Where is it?' he insisted.

'I'll get it for you.'

'You're not going anywhere.'

'It's here – over here.' She walked across to an old shoe box, opened it and pulled out a bundle of notes.

'Bring it over here,' he demanded, but even as he spoke there was a pounding of feet down the corridor.

'Hurry!'

She practically threw it into Angel's hands and he grabbed it, shoving the bundle into his jacket pocket.

'That makes two and a half grand and I've got it,' he jeered at Ed. 'I'm going to the South of France.' The smile had gone and only the sulky, beaten little boy was there, but nevertheless Jane could sense that he was desperate.

'That's not very nice,' said Gary suddenly.

'You shut up for a start.'

'You shouldn't hurt people.'

'You come anywhere near me and I'll cut her throat. Understand, wooden top?'

'Wooden top,' said Gary curiously. 'What exactly does *that* mean?'

At that moment two policemen burst into the room, one holding a flashlight.

'Don't come any closer,' said Angel slowly and

quietly. 'You can see how things are. I'm walking out of the room with the girl. Touch me and I'll kill her. I mean it.'

'I know you mean it, son,' said one of the policemen. He stood back and so did his colleague. 'Just take it easy.'

'I will. I want a car.'

'That won't be —'

'I want a car. Get it for me, or she dies.'

'All right, son,' said the policeman. 'Just take it very easy,' he repeated.

'Sure I will. And I'm taking her.'

'Where?'

'Up to the roof. Once I see the car in position I'll come down. Right?' Angel pushed the numbed Jane before him.

'Are we going to Margate now?' asked Gary.

'This kid trying to be funny?' asked the other policeman furiously.

'No,' said Mrs Lamb quickly. 'He's autistic.'

'Eh?'

'It doesn't matter. Just don't pay any attention to him.'

Gary looked at Mrs Lamb thoughtfully as if he hadn't quite understood what she had said but didn't like it anyway. Meanwhile Angel and Jane were out in the corridor, walking in the opposite direction to the front door. Then Angel paused and shouted back to Mrs Lamb, 'Oi – old lady.'

'What do you want?'

'How do you get on the roof?'

'You can't,' she said.

'You lie and you know what'll happen to the girl. I know you can get on. Now, how do you do it?'

Mrs Lamb said nothing, Ed shrugged, the two policemen looked uneasy and Gary merely curious, as if they were all trying to solve a rather interesting problem.

'Can you see Margate from the roof of this house?' he asked.

'Tell me,' yelled Angel.

'All right. Climb up the staircase to the top and there's an extending ladder to the loft. Go up to the loft and you can get out on the roof from there.'

'Come on then. Move.' Angel clattered down the corridor, pushing Jane in front of him. She noticed that in his desperation he seemed far less shaken now. However badly hurt, Angel had a purpose and Jane was quite sure that he was going to fulfil it. Suddenly the numbness dropped away and she began to shake in every limb.

Chapter
Eighteen

'We've got to get to Margate. We've got to get there in the morning.' Gary was becoming very agitated.

'Wait a minute –' said one of the policemen to Ed, who was moving towards the door. 'Where the hell do you think you're going?'

'I can talk him down,' said Ed. 'I've known Angel since he was six years old.'

'That doesn't mean –' began the policeman.

Ed ran off so fast that he took both policemen by surprise and, quick as a flash, Gary followed.

'Come back,' yelled one of the policemen.

'Gary, come back here at once,' shouted Mrs Lamb.

'No,' said Gary, his voice even as he almost overtook Ed. 'I'm afraid I can't come back. I've got to get to Margate.'

One of the policemen began to run down the corridor in pursuit but his colleague grabbed him. 'It's no good doing that – let 'em go.'

'They'll only complicate the whole damned issue,' he protested.

'Too bad. That guy Angel means business. I've seen that type before. Psychopath. He's really dangerous.

We have to get the whole emergency team in – fast. And he'll want to see that car.' He began to speak urgently into his radio and then he glanced up at Mrs Lamb, who was hovering by the door, looking indecisive.

'Madam,' he said. 'I hope you're not thinking of going anywhere.'

'But –'

'Because you're coming outside with us. This house will be surrounded by the incident squad any minute now and you must vacate immediately.'

'This is my home,' Mrs Lamb shouted at him but she knew that she would have to do as she was told.

'Go on.'

'I can't see.'

'Just go *on*.'

Jane struggled her way through the clutter, barging into old furniture and unidentifiable objects. Mrs Lamb seemed to have filled the loft with everything she didn't want – which was an awful lot – and the small space was jammed to the ceiling.

As Angel hauled himself up, Jane's eyes got used to the darkness and she could see there was a narrow, twisting path through all the jumble, towards a sky-light through which a pale beam of moonlight seeped.

'That's it.' He was breathing very heavily.

'What's it?' Jane knew what he meant but she wanted to misunderstand him as much as possible, to waste as much time as she could – anything to prevent them being out on the roof, just the two of them.

'There's steps up to the skylight.'

'Where?'

'You can see them.'

She could, and Jane stumbled over to them, hesitating at the bottom.

'Climb.'

'Suppose it's not open.'

'Climb.'

'I don't know *how* to open it.'

'Climb.' He was remarkably patient, considering the circumstances. 'I'll be right behind you.'

Jane climbed the dusty stairs and fiddled with the skylight. For a few seconds nothing happened and then suddenly it flew open.

'Move,' he said.

Jane climbed through, shivering in the chilly little breeze. Looking at her watch, she saw that it was almost four and there was no trace of dawn in the night sky. The remainder of the roof was flat, with a low stone balustrade running round the edge. She shivered again; how easy it would be to fall – or be pitched over the top. She glanced around wildly. Apart from a couple of chimneys there was no cover, no means of escape and clearly the skylight was the only way back. Angel hauled himself out and closed the hatch behind him. They were alone, up here, among the stars, but when she looked at him there was no terrible smile on his face – no trace of it at all. His thin features were screwed up in pain and the sweat was literally dripping off his forehead. A wild hope surged through her, but when she looked into Angel's eyes they were clear and determined and she knew that if she were to pit her wits against him, it was going to be a tremendous struggle.

*

They sat together against a chimney where Angel could see the skylight. Jane was conscious of vehicles arriving, people talking, radios chattering. There was a bustle and urgency below her but up here there was an eerie stillness. Then a searchlight flashed on and they were both flooded by sharp roving light.

As it came and went someone spoke on a tannoy. 'Angel. Come on, son. Give yourself up now. Don't get yourself into more trouble. It's only common sense.' The voice was benign and casual, almost like an uncle talking. Maybe it'll soon be like a father, thought Jane, with a flash of perception.

The amplified voice continued while the searchlight still swung round. 'It's not worth the hassle, Angel. Mr Parkinson, the man who owns the café, he's still alive and he's not on the danger list either. The hospital think he'll pull through. You're not going down for manslaughter, Angel. Let the girl go and come down and give yourself up. Drop the knife off the side of the building. We can come up to you if you like; we've got a turntable ladder down here – either way just take it nice and easy.'

The voice stopped and Jane was very relieved, for Angel was rigid with tension and even more sweat was pouring off his brow like a fast-flowing river. He began to mutter and then got up and staggered to the parapet. For a moment Jane wondered if he was going to throw himself off. Then she heard him shouting, 'Oi, you lot down there, where's my car? You promised me a car.' Realizing he had left Jane alone, he ran back to her in little limping strides, but he needn't have worried; she hadn't taken her opportunity to try to get back to the skylight – she was far too terrified to do that.

Angel dragged her to the drop and she stared down, amazed at what she saw below.

Around the revolving searchlight, which was mounted on the back of a truck, were a large number of police cars, a fire engine, another rescue vehicle with the revolving ladder and, most ominous of all, two ambulances. Curiously there was no sign of uniformed policemen or firemen. Only the man with the tannoy stood there and he was in plain clothes.

'Where's my car?' yelled Angel. He grabbed Jane and pushed her nearer to the drop. She felt sick with fright as she looked down, but her mind was crystal clear, racing now with ideas of escape that she rapidly rejected one by one.

The man with the tannoy lifted it to his lips. 'You take the girl in the car, Angel, and you're in big trouble. There'll be charges of abduction on top of everything else. Be sensible, son. Come down and talk this over with us. It'll go well with you if you can do that. Come down and show you can be trusted – show us you're not going to harm the little girl.'

'Go to hell,' spat out Angel and then, to her horror, Jane saw him relax. The smile appeared hesitantly, and then spread positively and calmly over his entire face, and as that smile returned so did her terror. Jane now knew that despite everything, Angel was back in his own deadly control.

'Get the car,' he called over the parapet. 'Get it now.'
    'This is a very bad move, Angel.'
    'I don't care about that. We're not playing a game.'
    'Angel, let's talk for a bit.'

'I'm not talking. I want that damned car – and I want it now. I want to see it. I want to see it now. And if I don't –' He pushed Jane even further towards the edge and as he held her, she felt her whole body shaking. 'If I don't I'll kill her. I'll push her over. Do you understand? Do you really understand?' All the time he was speaking, Angel's voice was cold and completely controlled. 'Do you understand?' he repeated.

'Yes,' said the man wearily. 'I understand.'

'Let me see the car,' commanded Angel. 'Turn the spotlight on it now.'

'OK.'

The spotlight revolved, contracted and picked out an unmarked Ford Escort standing just inside the battered gates of Mrs Lamb's house.

'Do you see it?'

'I see it,' said Angel.

But as he spoke, Jane heard another voice, clear as a bell under the night sky, toneless and piercing. 'This is a very long way round to Margate, isn't it?' Gary complained.

Ed tried to quieten him but it was too late.

Angel tightened his grip on Jane and shouted out, 'If anyone comes near me she goes over the edge, right?'

'Right,' said Ed.

'Keep that kid away from me.'

'OK.'

'And what the hell are you doing up here anyway?'

Jane's trembling was almost a convulsion now. The knife was in Angel's right hand, inches away from her throat, and she was terrified that he might suddenly lose control and stab her.

'Just came to talk to you,' said Ed gently. 'Try to make you see reason.'

'Reason – with that kid around?'

'He'll be fine. Hang around, Gary. We won't be long.'

'That's what everyone says,' protested Gary, 'but I've got to get to Margate.'

'If he ever mentions that name again,' said Angel through gritted teeth, 'I'll finish him off for sure.' He staggered slightly and Jane knew that he was weakening, that she had to bide her time. The trouble was that they were too near the edge for anyone to make many mistakes, and she hoped against hope that Ed wasn't going to. She was slightly reassured by the fact that Ed was watching Angel in a special way – full of awareness and compassion for the state he was in, but also appreciative of the fact that Angel was still a very dangerous opponent indeed. At least, that was Jane's interpretation, and she desperately hoped she was right.

'It's all right.'

'Stop being soothing,' snarled Angel. 'And what's that kid doing now?'

'Just mooching around.'

'Be careful,' said Jane. 'Please be careful, Ed. I don't suppose he's used to heights.'

Gary was exploring the roof, poking at broken slates and torn guttering.

'Careful, Gary,' said Ed. 'If you want to get to Margate in one piece, that is.'

'Are we going to Margate now?' asked Gary rather testily.

'Shut up!' screamed Angel and staggered again,

taking them both a little nearer to the edge of the roof.

'Watch what you're doing, Angel.'

'I am.'

'You heard what the plain-clothes guy said – Parkinson's alive.'

'They're just saying that – to trap me.'

'You sure?'

'Yeah, I'm sure.'

Ed stepped forward a little and Angel barked out, 'Stay where you are!'

'I want to talk.'

'Talk from there. But you've got nothing to say to me. Nothing at all.'

Ed stood his ground. 'Angel – this has all gone far enough.'

'With a liar like you. Yes.'

'I'm weak.'

'You can say that again.' But Angel's voice was shaking and his grip on Jane was loosening. She knew she still had to wait, however – wait until he really loosened his hold on her. If only Ed could keep him talking, make him more exhausted.

'But I'm trying to be strong now – trying to make you see sense.'

If only Gary doesn't interfere, thought Jane. If only he doesn't inevitably make some irritating comment or inquiry about Margate.

'The point is,' continued Ed steadily, 'if you go on like this you'll do a lifer. If you give up now they'll go easy on you. You know they will.'

'You *know* it makes sense,' sneered Angel, but by now his grip was so loose, so fragile, that Jane was determined to take her chance.

Chapter
Nineteen

'Hold it, you!'

Jane pushed, ducked, kicked, pushed again and almost broke free. Angel staggered this way and that, the knife waving haphazardly.

'Hang on,' yelled Ed and rushed forward.

'Keep away,' screamed Angel as he and Jane struggled, edging backwards towards the parapet. Suddenly she tripped, kicked and finally broke free, but instead of falling away from him, she fell sideways off the roof.

Had Jane pitched forwards, she would have fallen straight to the ground but she didn't. Instead she simply rolled over and grabbed the stonework, which left her dangling in space. Gradually she could feel her hands slipping on the damp surface, and as she yelled out piteously she could see that Ed was struggling to take the knife away from Angel and the only person who was near enough to help her was Gary – and Gary was deep in an intense game with broken tiles that he was piling one on top of another.

'Gary!'

He didn't look up.

'Gary!'

He still didn't look up.

'For God's sake – Gary!' Her hands were slipping even more now and she knew she only had seconds to go, but still Gary remained intent on the task in hand.

'Gary!' She knew she couldn't hold on much longer, and with a flash of inspiration she realized the words she should have used in the first place. If they didn't work now then she was finished. 'If you want to go to Margate – pull me up.'

'I'm busy.'

'Gary! Margate! You won't go if you don't help me,' she shrieked.

'You all keep saying we're going – then we don't,' he grumbled, placing a slate on top of his pile and looking round for another.

'The car's ready. We'll go now.'

'Where is it?'

'Look in the spotlight.'

'Where?'

'Down below.' Only her fingertips were holding her now. 'Hurry!'

'That's the car for Margate?' he said, looking down at the car that had been selected to placate Angel.

'Yes!'

'Where are you?'

'Hanging on down here.'

'What are you doing?'

'I fell over.'

'Fell over?'

'Gary!' she screamed. 'I'm falling. Don't you understand? I'm falling. You'll never get to Margate unless I'm with you, will you? Will you, Gary?'

'No – no I won't.'

'Grab my wrists now.'

He was with her in seconds and her wrists were locked into his strong, wiry grip.

'Pull,' she instructed him desperately. 'Pull.'

'Pull where?'

'Up!'

'You're heavy.'

'Pull!'

And pull he did. Slowly, bit by bit, Gary used his considerable strength to pull her back over the parapet.

Angel was lying on his back and Ed was kneeling on his shoulders. The knife was a few metres away from them, gleaming on the roof. Angel was shivering all over but he was quiet.

Jane, her whole body juddering from shock at the nearness of death, threw her arms round Gary and sobbed but he pushed her away. 'My arms hurt,' he grumbled. 'You're too heavy.'

'Thank you, Gary. Thank you.'

He returned to his tiles and continued to pile them up. 'We're going to Margate now,' he said, 'aren't we?' He added another tile, looking gloomy, as if he was convinced that whatever was asked of him, whatever he managed to do, there would still be delays.

'I'm sorry I couldn't help,' said Ed slowly. 'I didn't know what had happened until the last moment – not till I saw Gary pulling you up.' He grinned. 'Good thing I brought him up, wasn't it? He's a useful guy.'

Jane shuddered. 'After a bit of coaxing. I think the police are coming up; they must have had a good view of what happened.'

'Yes,' said Ed quietly. 'I guess they did. Angel's passed out, I think.'

'He looks terrible.'

'He's hurt bad – his head. I know he doesn't deserve to have anyone worried about him, but I am.'

Jane looked down at Angel's sweaty, waxen face. She couldn't hate him – not any more. 'Was he always like this? Violent? Main chancing?'

'Yes. Except when he was a little kid. He didn't stand much of a chance anyway.'

'Why not?'

'Mum a drunk. Dad too posh. He cleared off. That kind of sob-story – you know.'

Jane nodded. Yes, she knew that kind of sob-story.

'I tried to stick along with him – that's why I'm up here now. That's why I'm kneeling on his shoulders. Know what I mean?'

Jane nodded. She knew it all. Hearing the sound of pounding footsteps in the attic she went over to Gary, who appeared utterly absorbed in his construction.

'Will you be ready soon?' she asked.

'I'm busy,' he said crossly.

I wonder if I can really tell him we're going to Margate, Jane wondered, and then decided she couldn't, for there would be bound to be further delays now. She looked at Gary so busily employed. Was he just protecting himself from disappointment, or could he really just seal his mind off like this? On reflection she thought it was probably the latter.

As the policemen and firemen and the ambulance crews began to surge on to the roof-top, she stood by

Gary protectively. She didn't want him disturbed, not until the time had really come to make his momentous and much longed-for trip to Margate.

Chapter Twenty

An hour later, when Angel had been removed under police escort to hospital and Ed had been taken down to the police station, Mrs Lamb was at last given permission to drive Gary and Jane to Margate. Using one of the police telephones, Jane had spoken to her sleepy father and had tried to explain. In the end he had agreed that she could go, although he didn't really understand what was going on.

Surprisingly Mrs Bird had also agreed, although she too didn't really understand what had happened. 'He'll try to run away again,' she had said blearily to Jane. 'I know him. The police agree that your Mrs Lamb can be trusted so let him have a day with his dad, but I want him back by tonight and please will you ring me directly he arrives. I'm trusting you, mind.'

Jane had further reassured her and now here they were bumping up and down on the creaking springs of Mrs Lamb's car, which she drove through the early morning at a sedate thirty, oblivious to the traffic building up behind, trying unsuccessfully to overtake.

Gradually what had happened assumed the proportions of a distant nightmare and she began to doze as the Rover continued its stately progress down the motorway, although she was still conscious of Gary, sitting beside her, rigid with anticipation, his single-minded obsession now coming nearer and nearer.

'That sign says twenty-five miles to Margate,' said Mrs Lamb to Gary as Jane's eyelids drooped.

'Is that far?' he asked.

'Not very,' Mrs Lamb replied.

Gary looked at her suspiciously.

'We're here.'

Jane heard the sound of seagulls and woke up to see what she thought was one of the most wonderful sights she had ever seen. It was a golden morning and the Rover was running along the side of the esplanade at Margate, with the sea a winking silvery line, lapping at a vast expanse of damp sand. The tide was out and gulls wheeled and dipped over the beach.

Stiff and sore, her arms feeling as if they had been wrenched out of their sockets, her whole body bruised and weary, Jane nevertheless felt totally at peace with the world. It was almost as if she had finally arrived at a heavenly goal, for now they were at the end of Gary's quest and she felt like a knight returning at the end of a crusade.

Jane looked at her watch. It was just after eight and yet it felt much earlier. There were a few people walking their dogs on the beach, the traffic was light, there was no wind at all. In the glassy stillness it almost seemed as if the world had stopped turning and was taking a breather.

'What about getting some breakfast before we go to the house?' asked Mrs Lamb, huge and erect and majestic behind the wheel of her Rover.

'Are you hungry, Gary?' asked Jane.

'I'm hungry,' he said cautiously. She thought he looked tired and ominously rigid. They would have to be careful with him.

'We're in Margate now,' she said. 'We've arrived.'

'Dunroamin,' he muttered.

'How right you are,' put in Mrs Lamb, but he didn't understand her.

'It won't take long to get something to eat,' insisted Jane, for suddenly she was ravenously hungry.

'Supposing his father's gone to work?' asked Mrs Lamb anxiously.

'We know where he works, don't we, Gary? We know where your dad works.'

'At the Texas Steak House,' Gary said in a monotone.

'So we can track him down easily. Gary, you *must* be hungry.'

He nodded unwilling confirmation.

They had breakfast at an old-fashioned café on the seafront and Jane thought the meal was the most memorable she had ever had. Their plates were heaped with fried bread, bacon, eggs, tomatoes, sausages and mushrooms and there was as much hot buttered toast and strong tea as they could manage. Gary ate as ravenously as Jane and Mrs Lamb and when they were finally unable to manage any more, Mrs Lamb leant her vast bulk back on a tottering chair and said, 'What a blow-out.'

Gary began to tear a paper serviette into shapes – something that Jane had not seen him do before, but he seemed quite content.

'What will happen to Angel and Ed?' she asked Mrs Lamb.

'Well, Mr Parkinson is definitely going to get better – that's what the police said and I'm sure they're right. Even so, they'll be going away for a long time, especially Angel.'

'Ed was loyal to him –'

'Ed is weak,' Mrs Lamb pronounced. She shivered. 'The real world's all right for breakfast but not for much else, is it?'

'I don't know,' said Jane, staring thoughtfully at Gary. 'It's a very interesting place, isn't it? People are so different. At least – some of them are.'

'Are you sure this is the right place?' asked Jane as they drew up outside the council house.

'This is right,' said Gary happily, but Mrs Lamb and Jane looked at each other in a very meaningful way because there were no curtains at the windows and the front door was boarded up. Gary, however, didn't seem to notice and he leapt out of the Rover, calling out in joy, 'Dad – Dad, where are you? I've come home, Dad.' But all the time Jane could see that he wasn't really calling for his dad: he was looking inwards to himself. She could see that in his eyes, for she felt she was beginning to really know Gary now. Then she heard him muttering, 'Dunroamin – I want my Dunroamin, Dad.'

'I don't think there's anyone there,' whispered Mrs Lamb.

'His father must have moved.'

'But where?'

'I don't know,' said Jane. 'Let's hope it's not out of town. Anyway, we know where he works, don't we? The Texas Steak House.'

Gary had disappeared round the back of the house and Jane wondered whether she should follow him or not. She had a very nasty feeling that she was about to face one of Gary's greatest tantrums.

'What about asking *her*?' suggested Mrs Lamb.
   'Who?'
'The nosy neighbour.'
Jane hadn't noticed the woman come out of the next-door house and lean ominously over the fence. She wore a headscarf, boiler-suit and carpet slippers, and a cigarette was balanced precariously in the corner of her mouth.
'Excuse me,' said Mrs Lamb, looking very grand in her strange outfit.
'Yes?' Suspicious and unfriendly, the woman puffed acrid smoke at her.
'We're looking for a Mr Bird.'
'What do you want with him?'
'We've brought his little boy to see him.'
'The handicapped one?' she pronounced with relish.
'Er – yes.'
'Poor little mite,' she intoned sanctimoniously.
'What's happened?' asked Jane edgily and the woman looked at her with unexpected approval, as if she suddenly felt she was more her type.
'He's hopped it, hasn't he?'
'Gary's dad?'
'Yeah.'
'Where's he gone?' asked Jane anxiously.
'Gone up North.'
'Why?'
'Got himself a woman.'

There was a long silence, as if no more could ever be said. Then the woman surprisingly volunteered more, the cigarette still dropping out of the front of her mouth.

'Told me he'd write to Gary's mum with a new address.'

'Well, he hasn't done that yet.'

'Lazy blighter.'

Mrs Lamb instinctively kept quiet, knowing that she was unlikely to hit it off with the neighbour. Jane, meanwhile, knowing she did, tried another tack.

'I suppose – did you know he'd built a little house that Gary liked –'

'Dunroamin.' The woman gave a throaty chuckle. 'Yeah, he used to love that.'

'Do you know where it is?'

'I've got it.'

There was a long silence which was eventually broken by Mrs Lamb. 'Do you think we might buy it? I'll give you a good price.'

The woman frowned and Jane wished that Mrs Lamb had not spoken.

'I'm sorry,' Jane interposed quickly. 'I don't even know your name.'

'Ada Rankin.' She was slightly mollified. 'You don't need to buy Dunroamin off me.' Ada gave Mrs Lamb a nasty look. 'I was keeping it for Gary, wasn't I? It's in my back yard – under cover, mind. I've got it where my hubby keeps his bike.'

Jane leant over and kissed Ada on her powdered cheek.

'Thank you. Thank you so much.'

'That's all right, love.' Ada looked pleased.

'I'd better go and find Gary,' said Jane, disappearing down the alley between the houses and leaving Mrs Lamb and Ada Rankin to have a very awkward conversation indeed.

A howl of rage greeted her as Jane ran round to the back of the house and she saw Gary standing on the bare patch of earth that passed as a back garden, pummelling the locked back door.

'Dunroamin's in there,' he roared. 'Dunroamin's locked up.'

'No,' said Jane. 'Mrs Rankin's got it safe for you.'

'Mrs Rankin's got Dunroamin?' Gary turned to her, the rage draining out of his face. 'Mrs Rankin?'

'It's in the bike shed. Dunroamin's in the bike shed.'

He's going to hug me, thought Jane. At last he's going to hug me. Gary didn't. He just stared at her – but there was wonderment in his eyes. Although Jane knew that he didn't care for people, could never love anybody in the proper sense of the word and had been grieving for the absence of Dunroamin rather than the absence of his father, she took the initiative and threw her arms round him herself. At first he shrugged and she could feel his angry strength and was afraid, but the tighter she hugged him, the more relaxed he became.

NOTE

The Helen Allison School proposes to create a soft play area. Children with autism greatly benefit from the use of such an area. It allows them to release their tensions and anxieties in a safe and enjoyable way. The soft playroom can be used in conjunction with a behaviour management programme. If any readers of this book would like to send donations for this project to the Helen Allison School, the address is as follows:

The Helen Allison School
Longfield Road
Meopham
Kent
DA13 0EW